UNDER THREAT

A STRONG CURRENT TRILOGY BOOK 3

GREG OLMSTED

UNDER THREAT

A STRONG CURRENT TRILOGY BOOK 3

GREG OLMSTED

Library of Congress Control Number: 2015905325

ISBN 978-0-9861089-2-1 (trade paperback)

FIRST EDITION

Printed in The United States of America

Book design by Gwyn Kennedy Snider

*"Stewardship means that we weigh not only our own needs
and desires but those of other people and future generations.
We realize that none of us is a self-made person and that part
of what we own is wealth that flows from others through us.
We appreciate the natural resources, societal resources and
financial resources that have been handed down to us by our
ancestors and we are conscious of our own legacy."*
WWW.WISDOMCOMMONS.ORG

PART ONE
THE OIL SPILL

CHAPTER
ONE

THE YOUNG WOMAN, STANDING JUST INSIDE the front entrance of the department store, almost caught Keahi off guard. She smiled and offered her hand; he said hello and began to stop—did he know her?—and then he saw the bottle of perfume at her side like a pistol.

Keahi fought off a frown, for he didn't want to frown on Christmas Eve. But he detested the sweet smell of mixed perfumes that hung in the air: thick and overbearing. So he took a deep breath and quickly walked around her, detouring through the jewelry department.

He had just bought his last Christmas presents—bath oils for Carol and perfumed soaps for Angelica. He was also giving them a gift certificate for a night at the Royal Hawaiian. The older rooms in the hotel had large, old-fashioned bathtubs. Now he was negotiating his way through displays of jewelry, working his way towards an exit. *Soon,* he thought. *I'll be home soon. And then I'll have a couple of Foster's. After that, I'll wrap these presents and take them over to Carol and Angelica's.*

At the present moment, though, he found himself surrounded by the rustling of shopping bags, the clattering of leather shoes on flagstone, the bantering of last-minute shoppers perusing jewelry, crowding each other, brushing against each other. *This is crazy*, he thought. *Consumerism gone crazy.*

That's when he detected several kids stuffing their pockets with costume jewelry from display baskets set out on glass countertops. He watched their quick hands snatch the gaudy jewelry. He saw them deftly slip multicolored, sparkling bangles into the oversized pockets of their baggy jeans, exposing the elastic band of their underpants.

As he negotiated slowly through the crowd of shoppers and display tables, he saw a heavyset youth shuffling sideways between tables, crab-like, towards a revolving display case filled with gold earrings. His frayed cuffs scoured the flagstone.

He saw the youth's stocky body brush against an elderly Asian shopper, her upper body arched with age like a bow, her arms loaded with shopping bags. She tottered precariously. He expected her to fall; instead, she steadied herself with the heel of her hand, pushing off the top of a table. The table tilted and a glass menagerie of sea life on a mirror in the center of the table crashed to the gray flagstone. The long glass bill of a swordfish struck the mirror and snapped off. The mirror shattered. A hand-blown whale exploded against stone. An octopus lost its arms, the arms scattering in multiple directions. A hermit crab was crushed under the weight of its crystal shell.

"You should be ashamed, *tutu!*" the youth exclaimed, jumping away from the old woman and the broken crystal at her feet. He deftly passed the blame to her, raising his arms into the air, palms up. The expression on his face proclaimed, "It wasn't me!"

She started to scold him, but he placed his hands over his ears and shook his head vigorously, side-to-side. Then he turned his back to her and briskly stepped to the store exit and disappeared into a crowd of shoppers in the atrium of the mall.

Local punks, Keahi thought, as his Blackberry vibrated against his waist. *SH-HERC*, the display read. The State Hospital was calling out emergency responders to the Hawaii Emergency Response Center.

He speed dialed Jack but the connection went dead. *Damn!*

As he clipped the Blackberry back on his belt, one of the gang, who was still in the jewelry department, caught his eye and smiled nervously. *He must think I'm calling the police*, Keahi thought. The idea made him smile, too.

"Howzit, bruddah?" the punk asked as he cautiously slid by Keahi and exited the store, his eyes riveted on Keahi.

Keahi frowned, then exited, too.

The punk rendezvoused with another gang member and then glanced over his shoulder. When he saw that Keahi had also exited he yelled, "Go man, go!"

Keahi watched as they scurried like roaches down an up-escalator to a lower shopping level, disappearing from sight.

They think I'm after them, he thought with a half frown, as he walked briskly into the center of the atrium to get better reception. He speed dialed Jack again, the director of Hawaii's Department of Water, Wind and Sun.

"The State Hospital just texted. Unified Command is forming at the Response Center at Sand Island," Keahi spoke anxiously into his cell phone.

"I was called up too," Jack replied. "I'll meet you there, but I need to run an errand first." After a short pause he added, "You'll understand when I get there."

Fifteen minutes later Keahi arrived at the Response Center, a one-story white building off the Sand Island access road. A police met him at the entrance. The officer was a big-chested American-Samoan, as broad as Keahi, yet lacking Keahi's muscular density and six-foot-plus frame.

With one smooth motion, Keahi produced his picture ID and was allowed to enter. He shook the water off his umbrella and closed it, securing a Velcro strap.

"I'll take that," the police offered, taking the umbrella.

"Sure is a nasty night."

"Kona winds," the big man replied.

Keahi nodded agreement.

The police leaned the umbrella with others against the wall behind his gray desk, which was set in the back-center of the entry room. The desk served as a barricade to a hallway; any visitors to the Response Center had to negotiate both the big man and his large metal desk.

Keahi signed in and then stepped around the desk. He walked down the wide hall and turned left into the War Room. Oahu Civil Defense staff, dressed in Hawaiian shirts and blue jeans, were seated around a rectangular folding table, loudly talking on landlines. Across the room, a short, portly *haole* fed a multi-page message into a fax machine.

His face was familiar. He had a square jaw and bright, passionate eyes. His red hair was chopped short. It was Elijah.

Elijah worked for one of the major oil response companies based in Hawaii. Highly respected, his expertise included the strategic aspects of responding to oil spills, especially catastrophic oil spills. His resume included both the Valdez in Alaska and the Deepwater Horizon in the Gulf of Mexico. He had been prophesying for years about the inevitability of a catastrophic oil spill in Hawaii; for this reason the emergency responders fondly called him Elijah, even though his name was Eliot.

Even before Keahi sat down at the logistics table with the personnel from Oahu Civil Defense, he understood what had happened, and he needed no further explanation as to why he had been texted—there had been a catastrophic oil spill. It was reflected in the faces of everyone sitting around the table. He could see the tension in their faces.

Keahi glanced around the War Room. Everyone present knew each other on a first-name basis: they had spent considerable time preparing for tonight's event, conducting both tabletop and field exercises, and they knew each other's strengths and weaknesses. The guys from Civil Defense nodded and waved when they saw him, motioning for him to join them. They were obviously glad to see him.

But before he could start a conversation, Santos entered the room, huffing and puffing. Keahi was not surprised when the guys from Civil Defense rolled their eyes in dismay. Elijah's eyes rolled, too; Santos' reputation preceded him. He was an embarrassment.

Keahi sighed and drew his hands through his thick black wavy hair and shook his massive head. He took a deep breath and exhaled deeply. That sometimes helped.

He listened to the sounds around him. A fax machine shrilled an incoming call and then printed a message. A phone rang with a standard ring tone and a female voice answered: "Hello. Emergency Response Center." A page tore from a notepad. In the next room, voices marshaled, confident and authoritative. And the rain drummed on the metal roof overhead.

More responders arrived and took their places at four pre-assigned tables: logistics, plans, operations, general meetings. Then a Coast Guard representative read a roster of mustered personnel, and all present responded by replying, "Here."

When Jack's name was called and he didn't answer, Santos stepped forward and proclaimed that he was the department's Incident Commander, the guy in charge.

No one is impressed, Keahi thought as he surveyed the room. *But where IS Jack?*

Most of the players from the State had arrived: Keahi and Santos for the Department of Water, Wind and Sun; the Health Department; the State Civil Defense Agency, who coordinated the City and County of Honolulu's Public Works, Fire and Police Departments; the Harbor and Marine Patrol; and the Harbor's Division of the Department of Transportation. Among the federal personnel who answered roll call were those from the U.S. Fish and Wildlife, the National Marine Fisheries, and the Transportation Security Administration.

Now Keahi *knew* the spill was catastrophic because a half-dozen response contractors had been called in too, in addition to personnel from Naval Base Pearl Harbor, plus the U.S Navy Supervisor of Salvage.

The Coastie reading the roster made special note that a representative for the responsible party—that is, the party responsible for the oil spill release—was not present. Keahi wondered who they were. Did the incident involve a ship or a pipeline? If it was a ship, what kind? What was her name? How big was she? What had happened?

"It's still too early for the lawyers to show up," someone commented nervously.

"The responsible party may not have insurance, but they always have lawyers," someone added, trying to lighten the mood.

"Elijah, what have you heard?"

Elijah set his elbows on the table and clasped his hands together. "At 1917 hours this evening, the Coast Guard Group Honolulu received a distress call from a tanker, the Global Oil Achilles. Then all communication was lost."

There was silence around the table; everyone was attentive to Elijah's deep voice.

"Our file on the Achilles gives her breadth as 90 feet, depth 50 feet, draft 40 feet. She displaces 52,000 tons. She's a big girl. At this time, we don't know how many gallons of crude she was carrying. That's right—crude. Dirty oil."

"We do know, however, that fully loaded she has the capacity to carry 30 million gallons. She is fitted with 18 cargo tanks, arranged three across—one port, one center, one starboard—by six longitudinally. She is an old tanker. Her cargo tanks have no double bottom space beneath them." He paused, for effect, and then added: "That is *not* good."

"According to the last communication between the captain of the Achilles and the Coast Guard, her steering had failed and she was in our coastal waters, just off our reefs." Again he paused. "That *also* is not good."

"And worst of all, the captain of the Achilles said she had collided with a longliner. He said the longliner caught fire immediately after the collision. He heard a series of explosions, including one loud explosion, which I am sure you also heard. I heard it and I was at home watching the Clash of the Titans." He paused, smiled, then added, "At first I thought the explosion was Zeus throwing a thunderbolt."

Some in the room laughed, nervously.

Keahi thought to himself, *I must have been inside the department store.*

"The fire and the explosions may account for the fact that we are not able to establish communication with the longliner. So we have not yet identified her. Both ships were disabled about one mile off Barbers Point. And that, ladies and gentlemen, is all I know at this time."

"No prophecy, Elijah?" a hopeful voice asked.

"Prophecy?" Elijah repeated. "Well, I thought you might expect me to say something, so how about a passage from the Book of Job. It goes something like this:

If I had put my trust in tourists
or said to the tourists, 'You are my security,'
if I have rejoiced over my great wealth,
the fortune my hands had gained,
if I have regarded the sun in its radiance
or the northeasterly trades in splendor,
so that my heart was secretly enticed
and my hand offered them a kiss of homage,
then...

"That describes our current situation very well," Elijah said.

"But what does it mean?" a representative from the Harbor's Division asked.

"It means Job had better standing with God than us," Elijah said. "And we know what happened to Job, don't we?"

"It's going to be a long night," someone mumbled.

"Howzit?" a voice asked behind Keahi.

He recognized the voice even before he turned around, and he broke into a big grin. "My God, Pete! It's good to see you."

Keahi stood up and they embraced in a hug and patted each other on the back.

"What are you doing here?" Keahi asked. Pete had resigned from the department about a year ago, following an explosion during a meth lab investigation that had killed a coworker.

"This is what I live for," Pete replied, matter-of-factly. Then as an afterthought: "Where's the pizza?"

"You arrived before we ordered," Keahi said, smiling.

Several responders came over and warmly greeted him. "Glad to have you aboard," one of them said.

Santos's reaction, however, was not friendly. "How did you get in?" he demanded. "This is a restricted area. Only members of the response team are allowed."

"The old ID still works." Pete grinned and tapped the baby blue-colored ID clipped to his shirt pocket. Silver hologram stars and hologram sunbeams sparkled on the ID, which carried the following notice to civil authorities: *Please permit the EMERGENCY WORKER identified by this card to his/her duty station.*

"I'll see about that," Santos said as he disappeared through a door to the hallway and immediately returned with the police.

"Mr. Baniaga here says you entered without a valid ID," the police inquired. "Is that correct, sir?"

"Yes," Pete answered.

"You will have to come with me, sir."

"I understand." Pete leaned over and read the policeman's name badge. "You're doing a good job, Officer Bautista, but I have no intention of leaving. You see, I'm needed here."

"Santos," Keahi said, "he's right. We *are* going to need his help."

"Officer," Santos paused to catch his breath. He was out of shape. Overweight. His girth was larger than the Samoan-American, but it was all fat. He was short, barrel-chested and fat. Just racing up the hall to get the police had winded him. "I expect . . ." He lost his breath. "I expect . . ." He started making puffing sounds.

The policeman looked at Pete, judging his size. Pete was just average build, except for his broad shoulders.

"Sir, either you leave now or I take you into custody."

"Actually, I have permission to be here."

"Really?" Santos said to Pete. He turned to the police. "Officer?"

Keahi felt embarrassed for the department. It was business as usual.

The police reached behind his back and pulled a set of handcuffs off his belt. He opened one cuff and said, "Sir, please turn—"

"What's going on here?" Jack interrupted. He walked across the room, pushing through the tight group of responders surrounding Santos and Pete, and confronted the police. Jack was a short, gray-haired old man with a willowy frame, standing toe-to-toe with a police three times his size.

The room grew still.

"He's arresting me for trespassing."

"He no longer works for the Department," Santos declared. "He's not authorized to be here."

"I apologize for arriving late," Jack said, addressing everyone in the War Room, "but I had an errand to run first. And I had to phone the head of our personnel and get her approval to rehire Pete as an Emergency Hire. I called Pete en route and gave him the news. And then when I got here, it took forever to find a parking place."

Jack put his hand on Pete's shoulders. "We wouldn't go into this response without the best players on our team, would we?"

"No sir," Pete said, smiling.

Several Coasties nodded approval in unison. Having Pete back on the team was an immediate boost to the *esprit de corps.*

"Sorry sir," the police said to Pete. He turned sharply and left the War Room.

"Santos," Jack said, "we need to talk."

The room grew silent.

Santos shook his head in disbelief.

Jack led Santos to an unoccupied corner of the room and then turned to face him squarely. "I suggest you go home," Jack said. "Get some rest. We will need you for the next shift."

"I'm not tired," Santos protested.

Keahi could hear the rain beating against the roof.

"This is not a request, Santos."

Bristling with indignation, Santos turned and lumbered across the War Room, the rubber soles of his field boots squeaking across the tiles. He passed through the door, mumbling and wheezing.

"Must be sleepwalking," one of the Coasties said, his voice loud enough for everyone to hear. They all laughed at that, and the mood in the War Room improved considerably.

Three big points for Jack, Keahi thought. *And if this emergency is as bad as I think it is going to be, we'll need all the good will we can muster.*

Jack introduced himself, again joking about the inadequate parking—it had taken ten minutes to find a parking place—and then he asked for an update.

The Coasties told him about the Global Oil Achilles and the longliner. Elijah, nearby, listened and nodded.

"Sir, I'll show you to the Unified Command Room, sir," Pete said to Jack.

When they were out in the hallway, Jack said, "Please, don't call me sir."

"That's for the Coasties' benefit."

"I see," Jack said, reluctantly. "But only until this crisis is over. Is that understood?"

"I have a feeling that *that* is going to be a long time."

Jack studied Pete's face for a moment, then stepped back into the War Room and signaled Keahi to join them. "Is there a place we can talk in private?" Jack asked.

"The library," Pete said, "farther down the hall to the left."

Once the three of them were inside, Jack pushed the library door closed. "What is the department's level of preparedness?"

"We're not," Pete answered.

"During the field exercises, my role was the operations and planning chief," Keahi volunteered.

"And you, Pete?"

"Sir, until you joined the department, I played your role, the Incident Commander. The previous Head of Department . . . well, he was a crisis manager, not a believer in proactive emergency preparedness. He never attended exercises, sir."

"I see," Jack said. "Pete, I'd like you to be my second-in-command—the department's Deputy Incident Commander."

"Yes, sir. What's our first assignment?"

"Do we have staff who can help with this emergency?"

"Yes, sir," Keahi said, grinning. "Our new team. Collectively, they have expertise in air, water, hazardous substances—including oil—and solid waste."

"Very good. Keahi, I need you to call them out. Peter, I need you to prepare duty assignments. Any questions?"

Keahi and Pete looked at each other. "No, sir," they said in unison.

"Then let's shine."

Keahi thought 'let's shine' was an unusual thing to say, given the nature of their current situation: bad weather, ships colliding, ships burning, and all of that happening the week of Christmas. And it was nighttime.

Jack opened the library door and they stepped back into the hallway. Pete and Keahi watched him walk up the hall. He joined the command staff in the Unified Command room at the front of the building, near the entrance and the police guard.

And then Keahi followed Pete back into the library. Pete leaned against one of the bookcases, then turned to Keahi and said, "Who's on this team of yours? What are their skills?"

"What skills do you need?"

"Well, the diesel from the longliner is burning, so we need air monitoring. When people wake up tomorrow morning, they'll be bitching about burning eyes and scratchy throats. And we may decide to torch the crude. That could send every asthmatic in the islands to the emergency room."

"Torch the crude?"

"Hell, we may torch the crude *and* the Achilles. But first, someone's got to assure us that the wind is blowing in the right direction and at the right speed—away from Oahu."

"And if the wind changes?"

"Then the public will kick our ass."

"Well, Kwon is in the air unit," Keahi said.

Pete's blue eyes studied Keahi. He nodded. "I also need a hazardous waste expert. Someone who knows how to dispose of thousands of tons of oil-contaminated debris."

"That would be Masako."

Pete stared at Keahi in disbelief.

"She's sharp."

"I heard that Kwon and this Masako dislike each other." When Keahi didn't say anything, Pete added: "I don't want problems. If they can't check their personal baggage at the door, then tell them to stay home."

"That's Jack's job," Keahi said.

Pete frowned. "He won't have the time. I also need a biologist, someone who can work with the whale watchers. We will have dead fish washing ashore, and we will have oiled birds and turtles to rescue."

"Toi," Keahi volunteered. "She has a degree in marine biology."

"Good," Pete said. "I'll take surveillance and track the oil spill."

Keahi thought about that. "Okay, and what about me?"

"We need an operations chief. That's you. Make sure we have equipment, supplies—that kind of thing."

"What? You get to fly in the helicopter and I get to grunge around looking for booties?"

Pete gave Keahi a big smile. "I'll take you up with me." He patted Keahi on the shoulder.

"And the first thing you need to do is order pizzas," he added. "Aren't you hungry?"

"Listen up," a Coastie called out loudly so he could be heard above the multitude of feverish conversations taking place in the War Room. He walked over to the weather report board and erased some old information.

"We're at the beginning of a winter Kona squall: cloudy skies, heavy rain showers. The sea's from the south with eight- to twelve-foot swells." The white chalk scratched as he wrote '8 to 12 foot' on the green board.

"Kona winds are moving in a southwesterly direction. An advancing cold air front has encountered a slow-moving, warm air mass rising above it. We expect continuous rain. This is a big front, over 200 miles wide, with 25-knot winds and occasional 70mph gusts over land."

"Tonight's weather will be with us for several days. Kona winds are expected to increase to 40 knots." Chalk scratched again as the Coastie described the flood and ebb of the tides, and the currents along the coastline.

He ended on a light note. "Two things we know for sure: the weather is going to get worse, and the sun will rise in the morning. We may not see it, but the sun will be there."

All eyes turned to the front of the room as the Federal On-Scene Coordinator, the U.S. Coast Guard Captain of the Port, Captain Burke, entered and cleared his throat.

"At 1917 hours this evening, Captain Lycusgus, the captain of the tanker Global Oil Achilles, contacted Coast Guard Group Honolulu and reported his tanker had collided with a longliner. As the primary responder for at-sea oil spills, and because the owners of the Global Oil Achilles failed to provide an adequate response, the U.S. Coast Guard has assumed full responsibility."

Keahi thought of the old expression, *shoot first and ask questions later.*

"At 1930 hours, within minutes of losing communications with the Achilles, I directed the U.S. Coast Guard Cutter Harrison to get underway to the scene of the collision. A short time later, a second U.S. Coast Guard Cutter also responded."

"The Coast Guard 14th District Office contacted Navy Pacific Headquarters and requested Navy Salvage resources." The captain paused and acknowledged a representative of the Navy Supervisor of Salvage, seated at the operations table.

"At 1939 hours, 22 minutes after our first communication with the Achilles, a Coast Guard aircraft was airborne en route to the scene from Coast Guard Air Station Honolulu."

"At 2027 hours, one hour and ten minutes after the incident was reported, a Coast Guard team, at great personal risk to themselves, rescued several crew members from the waters surrounding the longliner."

"Several of the longliner crew are still missing. Crew who were rescued described other crew who did not make it off the longliner. The collision, the fire, the smoke, the explosions—all these hazards may have trapped some crew."

"I'll now turn the briefing over to Officer Jamison for a more thorough report on the fire."

Officer Jamison, a younger man than Captain Burke, was also his physical opposite—tall, pale and blond.

"The Navy salvage team tried to suppress the fire aboard the longliner, with the Cutter Harrison nearby. Unfortunately, our salvage vessels were unavailable to respond due to assignments elsewhere, so we responded with the best available, a local tug, Kroll, which was recently outfitted with a remote controlled monitor. She suppressed the flames surrounding the longliner long enough for several crew to be rescued. However, the Kroll provided only temporary relief and the longliner is still burning."

After a thorough accounting of the sea rescue, Officer Jamison turned the briefing back to Captain Burke.

"Besides the fire on the longliner," Captain Burke said, "our other immediate concern is the disabled tanker, Achilles." The captain paused and rubbed his chin. "We are not sure if we have sufficient tug power to bring her in safely . . . or, alternately, to keep her off our reefs.

"At this time we do not know how many of her tanks are damaged, so prepare for a worst-case oil spill. Any questions?"

Someone asked, "Sir, how bad is it, sir?"

"I personally believe that this spill will be worse than the Exxon Valdez."

And it will happen right here in the waters off Hawaii, Keahi thought.

An hour later Keahi had contacted his team members and directed them to report immediately to the command center. He then made the rounds to each of the tables in the War Room. Finishing with the table designated for the planners, he stopped and asked Elijah, "Any new reports?"

"Most of the longliner crew is missing," Elijah said. "As for the Achilles, the Coast Guard was unable to lighten her."

"Really? What happened?"

"You know there is not a standard package of oil transfer equipment that works for all vessels? Well, the Coast Guard did not have the reducers and adapters they needed to connect hoses between their ships and the Achilles." Elijah shook his head in dismay. "A very simple but insurmountable problem when you're out in the Pacific, without easy access to your local naval supply store. As a result, they are unable to lighten the tanker as much as they would like. And with this Kona storm, anything can happen."

"What about towing her out to sea?"

"Nope," Elijah commented. "Not enough tug power. Look out the window. A fierce storm is building up. The Achilles will either spill her load just off the coast, or she will drift in and break up on our reefs. Either way, it will be ugly."

"Is Waikiki going to be oiled?" Keahi asked. Several emergency responders had gathered around and were listening attentively to Keahi and Elijah's conversation; everyone wanted more information.

Having an audience, Elijah prophesized. "Because the Achilles is so close to shore and because nighttime response is so hazardous, the Coast Guard has few options. So far, attempts to lighten and tow her have failed. It does not matter much if she breaks her back at her current location, or if her tanks rip open on our reefs. Either way, crude oil will strike the south shore like a single wave assault. Some of it may sink, but most of it will wash ashore. Crude will spread around to our east and north shores, just like an invading navy."

"So Waikiki will be seriously impacted," Keahi stated.

"There is some good news," Elijah continued. "A significant portion of the crude oil may bypass Oahu."

"But that crude oil will be carried westward and will wash ashore on Kauai," Jack said. "And the Northwestern Hawaiian Islands will be oiled, too."

"Well, that's the bad news," Elijah said.

"Goodbye monk seals," someone said.

"Probably so," Elijah concurred, his voice sad. "The seals' population is too small to survive. The stress of this oil spill will push them over the edge into extinction."

CHAPTER TWO

ON THE MORNING OF THE FIRST DAY, Keahi sat nervously in a Coast Guard helicopter, his hands wrapped around a venti coffee. Pete, in contrast, was thrilled and it showed in his eyes. They had caught a temporary break in the heavy rainfall and the sun was shining. It was like being in the eye of a storm. Buckled into their seats, they hovered above the longliner, surveying the damage caused by her collision with the Achilles. A devastating fire had swept through the commercial fishing vessel. Keahi gazed at her scorched remains, held in place by a tug and surrounded by blackened flotsam.

A Coast Guard cutter was anchored a safe distance away, riding rough waves. Keahi spotted a rescue raft secured alongside the longliner. A Coast Guard rescue team had braved the choppy waves.

The helicopter thundered above the longliner. Keahi watched two orange jumpsuits appear topside, carrying a bagged body on a stretcher. They set the yellow bag next to three other body bags, forming a solemn row on the starboard deck. Then the two men looked skyward and waved at the Coast Guard helicopter—at Pete, Keahi, and the pilot. After that they carried the stretcher below deck again.

"They're recovering bodies now," Pete said. "After the fire burned out last night—by itself, I might add—the Coast Guard hosed her down for two hours and then lightened her of any remaining diesel fuel. When they finish recovering bodies, that tug will push her out to sea and they will scuttle her."

The pilot turned in his seat and spoke to Pete. "Sir, we need to clear this air space. A helicopter is approaching to airlift the bodies." The pilot was an Asian man of indeterminate age, with a severe, closed face.

"Take us to the Achilles," Pete ordered, raising his voice above the thunder of the rotors. "I'd like to see the Achilles."

"Sorry sir, can't take you there at this time. News helicopters flying around the Achilles like vultures on a dead cow. Until we reestablish air space, we can't risk going in there, sir."

"Flying cockroaches," Keahi muttered, remembering the newscasters who had televised Kwon's bloody exit from the pet store.

"Someone will lose their pilot's license, sir," the pilot said to Keahi.

"I hope so." Then Pete suggested, "Let's survey the coast from Tracks Beach to Makapuu Point. Track the oil along the shore."

"Yes, sir," the pilot said, obediently swooping northeast towards Barbers Point.

"Did I tell you about the collision between the Greek vessel Likoia and the Singaporean vessel the Enif?" Pete asked Keahi.

"No."

"It happened at midnight, off the coast of Louisiana in the Gulf. The vessels locked together. Three tugs pushed them to deeper waters, where the plan was to first lighten them, then pull them apart."

"What happened?"

"The weather was too severe to lighten them, but they pulled the vessels apart anyway—on the fourth of July. When it was all done, the Enif had spilled her oil."

"I'm glad you're back," Keahi said.

"So am I." Pete smiled.

As the helicopter approached the coast, Keahi recognized two dull-gray, concrete stacks and three concrete buildings that loomed arrogantly in front of the yellow-brown Waianae hills. It was the Hawaiian Electric Plant.

A four-lane black top, Farrington Highway, lay like a snake in front of the power plant—a black racer snake with a white stripe down its back, wrapping itself along the coastline. Power poles and lines, blown over by high wind gusts, lay across the blacktop, giving the appearance of a snake caught in a net. Eerily, there was no traffic.

The helicopter hovered just off shore, overlooking the inlet for the Hawaiian Electric Plant and Tracks Beach. Huge waves pounded the wide beach; buffeted by the Kona storm, the waves were three times their normal size. Mean and deadly.

If we crash, Keahi thought, *those waves will grind us into hamburger.* His breakfast rose to the back of his throat and he felt stomach acid burning his esophagus. *Hell, when the rotors hit those waves....* He wished he had a Zantac. He secured the lid on his hot coffee.

"The easterly currents must have carried the oil away from this area, away from the power plant and Tracks Beach," Pete said.

"That's a good thing," Keahi said. "Waves are crashing over the breaker wall that surrounds the inlet to the electric plant."

Pete nodded concurrence.

Next, they flew south along the rocky coastline to the Ko'Olina resort. The four man-made lagoons and small crescent beaches had been spared. The horseshoe-shaped sandy beaches shone bright white. And the ocean water, as it circulated in and out of the lagoons through narrow entrances built into the rock barrier walls, sparkled clean. As a precaution, though, orange booms had been strung across the narrow entrances to prevent oil from entering. The sections of orange boom floated like pieces of gigantic *ilima* lei, Keahi thought.

Just south, the deep-draft harbor and private marina were also, so far, untouched by the crude.

Suddenly the pilot rose fifty feet straight up, providing Pete and Keahi a spectacular view. The artificial ponds in the Ko'Olina golf course glistened as they reflected the early morning sunlight: shining pearls in a green oasis in a brown landscape. In the distance, the sleepy residents of Makakilo, on the slopes of the Waianae Range, were just waking up.

The helicopter flew further south along the coastline to Campbell Industrial Park, Hawaii's only heavy industrial park, where two oil refineries were busy converting crude oil into gasoline. The old Chevron refinery was on the west side of the park, near the coast. On the east side, a multitude of aboveground storage tanks rose from the ground like white pustules waiting to rupture.

Through the years, Keahi had responded to dozens of complaints and emergencies within this park arising from myriad chemical releases. But today, the beaches on the west and south shores had been spared an oil slick; the currents were carrying the oil to the east, away from the industrial park.

And that is the direction they flew—eastward along the coast, directly into the early morning sun. Pete missed nothing. He was enjoying the flight. Keahi, in contrast, now had stomach gas: sudden fifty-foot changes in altitude set poorly with his dense, muscular body. The flight was fatiguing him. He felt a headache starting above his right eye.

Seated behind Pete, Keahi admired his wavy brown hair and his broad shoulders. *My God, he's handsome.*

Pete had been his mentor and his best friend at work, with the possible exception of Kwon in the air unit. Keahi had worked side-by-side with Pete for all these years, at least until the meth lab explosion.

The meth lab explosion had been a serious setback for Pete. He had been bruised from head to toe, and his back-up responder, Little Bill, had died from concussive injuries.

Keahi recalled how the tragedy had devastated Pete. Burdened by remorse and guilt for Little Bill's death, he abandoned his job. He just walked into work, told off their boss Santos and quit.

That same morning he gave Keahi his collection of petroleum samples from dozens of petroleum releases throughout the islands. But most importantly, he gave Keahi his most prized possession: a fuel oil sample from the U.S.S. Arizona, the fuel that was slowly releasing from the sunken ship into Pearl Harbor, the fuel that created the beautiful rainbow sheen on the ocean surface at the memorial. After giving the small glass vial of petroleum mixed with seawater to Keahi, Pete had said goodbye and walked out.

Their boss, Santos, had assigned Keahi several of Pete's cases, including the fire and explosion at a child care center playground that had injured two children. It was a difficult case for Keahi to take over, especially since Pete had quit and wasn't there to hand off the case. And that upset Keahi.

After quitting, Pete had rented a room on the north shore where he rode the waves and worked part-time at a shrimp truck selling plate lunches. When he wasn't in the water he indulged his passion for hiking.

Months passed before they saw each other again. Not surprisingly, they met at an emergency response scene. Keahi was the emergency responder, Pete, an observer. Pete had been listening to the emergency channels on his radio scanner when he heard the dispatch for a fire at a nearby laboratory. He just had to check it out. It was so close and someone may have needed his help. But it was just an empty building, a laboratory going up in flames. Together they had watched the blaze.

And now they were together in a helicopter. Pete was living in the moment, having jumped right back into the work that he loved. Keahi, on the other hand, was stressed out.

It was at Oneula Beach Park that they first saw light traces of oil reflecting the sunlight. By the time they reached Ewa Beach, the coast was awash in black oil.

They hovered directly offshore from Ewa Beach for what seemed an eternity, Keahi thought, as the pilot waited for approval from air traffic control to approach the runway reef on the south side of Hickam Air Force Base and the Honolulu International Airport.

As they waited, Keahi felt a pang of sadness as the first effects of the oil spill began to register in his mind. As a youngster, he had picked *limu* at Ewa Beach and up and down this coast. But because of overharvesting and non-point source runoff from the surrounding houses, which had been built on formerly fertile sugarcane fields, the *limu* had almost disappeared. After today, though, the oil would smother any remaining seaweed.

The beach was deserted.

"They have already set up a security area below us, starting at the western fringe of Ewa Beach." Pete pointed to several camouflage-painted trucks and a Humvee. "There, where all the military vehicles are parked."

"The National Guard is setting up a safety zone from here all the way to Diamond Head. The National Guard will control the shore and the Coast Guard will patrol the water along the coast to protect anyone foolish enough to venture out into this black shit."

It appeared to Keahi that the cleanup started here, too, and expanded to the east. "Masako is somewhere down there, isn't she? Setting up staging areas for oil-soaked debris?"

Masako and Kwon, Keahi thought. *They are as compatible as oil and water.* Whenever they got together it wasn't a pretty sight. He shook his head. What was Kwon's problem? Why was he so aggressive when he was around her? Why so intense? Why so argumentative? He shook his head again, but this time in bewilderment.

"It's hard to imagine that this was a pretty beach," Pete said, his voice sad. "No one will be using those picnic tables for a long time."

Keahi saw three green recycled plastic tables under the shade of the trees. They looked small and misplaced.

"Sir, we have approval to approach the reef runway," the pilot said, darting up the coastline to Iroquois Point. "We can view the area for four minutes. We have two minutes in and two minutes out."

When they reached the entrance to Pearl Harbor, Keahi saw that the Navy's best efforts had been mocked by high winds. "The oil is passing over the booms on the larger waves," Keahi said.

"It's also being pushed under the booms, rolling just below the surface with the surge," Pete said, expanding on Keahi's observation.

Next, they flew across the harbor entrance and hovered close to the water's surface at the eastern end of the reef runway.

"Can submarines navigate through oil?" Keahi asked.

"Sir," the pilot said, "I understand that the submarines moved to open ocean before the oil impacted this area."

"The Navy probably alerted the Submarine Base before they dispatched the cutters to help the Achilles," Pete speculated.

"National defense *is* their number one priority," the pilot offered.

"Looks like the oil has mixed into the mudflats fronting Fort Kamehameha Beach," Keahi observed.

"How will they ever clean that up?" the pilot asked.

Keahi and Pete didn't reply; the area would have to be dredged.

Below them a small remnant of reef, one that had survived numerous environmental catastrophes in the past, now lay beneath a heavy layer of black oil, smothered. It had survived the dredging of the harbor entrance, the scalping of the coral flats to develop Hickam Beach and Hickam Boat Harbor, the silt and chemical contaminants that had drained through three man-made drainage canals from Hickam Air Force Base into Mamala Bay. But now, the small reef lay buried in oil.

Keahi sensed that the fate of the marine life inside the harbor would be no better. The Navy had tried to boom Pearl Harbor and Bishop Point and Hickam Harbor, but their efforts had failed. The weather and the ocean now controlled the oil.

If the Navy can't protect Pearl Harbor, Keahi thought, *what will happen to Waikiki?*

The acid in his esophagus was still there, burning a hole in his chest and neck.

Keahi saw that the estuary between the runway reef and the coastline along Hickam Air Force Base had filled with oil. "At least the booms on the reef are working well," Keahi said, sarcastically, "diverting oil into the estuary." He had known that the estuary would be sacrificed to collect oil; nevertheless, seeing it filled with oil filled him with a dark, directionless anger.

"Yes, the estuary runneth over," Pete said, sadly agreeing with Keahi's observation.

"Sir," the pilot said to Pete, "we need to leave the area before a 767 arrives."

"Can you fly us over Honolulu Harbor?" Pete asked.

"Yes, sir."

They left the reef runway and flew towards Honolulu, passing south of Keehi Lagoon and Sand Island. Because of the rough seas, the attempt to boom Keehi Lagoon for near shore containment and oil recovery had failed. From their viewpoint, seventy feet above the ocean, they could see that Honolulu Harbor had been oiled, heavily.

Keahi watched as black, contaminated waves pounded the white sides of a cruise ship anchored at the Aloha Tower tourist complex. The foul waves licked the ship, staining her a dirty yellow-brown.

Behind the commercial complex, the massive towers of the federal building resembled two washboards set upright. At the mouth of Nuuanu Stream, fresh water was mixing with black oil, creating a gray froth. Oil washed against piers and onto ships, which had anchored in the harbor for safety from the storm.

To the west, a gigantic deepwater barge, loaded with white and red shipping containers, was anchored adjacent to the Sand Island Container Terminal. Huge yellow cranes on the shore towered above the shiny black sheen.

The bright yellow cranes and the white tanks contrasted against the black oil, and reminded Keahi of a van Gogh painting, the yellow and white suggesting intensity, vehemence. If you stepped into one of his paintings, Keahi thought—if you found yourself in his painting of a poolroom, or an outdoor café, or his famous starry night—you might go mad. Now looking at the harbor area, with the early morning sun glistening off the crude oil, Keahi felt a shudder climb his back.

They flew on towards Waikiki, flying parallel to the large boulders along the long seawall fronting Kakaako Park. Waves were splashing over the top of the ten-foot seawall, and dirty, oil-laced spray was blowing into the park, streaking the sides of the green hills black. Just last week Keahi had watched school kids sledding down these grassy hills on brown cardboard cut from shipping boxes. Today, the park was empty.

As they flew on, passing Kewalo Basin and the charter fishing boats, Keahi struggled to process the barrage of terrible images bombarding his nervous system. Everywhere he looked, he saw black oil washing ashore.

Tears welled up in his eyes as the helicopter flew parallel to Ala Moana Beach Park. He saw the crude oil lying on top of the beach and guessed that several inches had probably collected at the bottom of the man-made channel, where he had swum laps almost every afternoon. His lazy afternoons, swimming here during lunch, were gone.

It was at Waikiki that he noticed the television reporters. They had set up their cameras with the waning sunrise in the background, and they were scurrying about, taking shots of the oil washing up on the narrow, eroded, man-made beaches of Waikiki and the hardened seawalls.

"I can hear them now," Keahi said, his voice mimicking a local newscaster. "We have lost the battle for the south shore." Then he tapped Pete on the shoulder and pretended to hand him a microphone. "And now, back to you Danno for the local news."

"The oil is expected to flow easterly, influenced by both the currents and the tides," Pete said, turning around in his seat to face Keahi, pretending to be a reporter. "According to the Coast Guard, the low tide impacts will be the worst. And warning signs will be posted everywhere: CAUTION! SLIP-PERY WHEN OILED!"

CHAPTER THREE

ON THE MORNING OF THE SECOND DAY, as the sun rose but failed to shine on Hanauma Bay, Toi observed the destruction. She stood at the top of the extinct volcano and looked down into the rusty-colored cauldron, breached on one side, filled with black bile. The one-lane asphalt road, steeply graded from the top of the volcano to the beach, far below, looked like the handle of a scythe. The crescent-shaped beach along the inner edge of the bay was the long, curved blade, and it was smeared with black oil.

Her eyes searched for the keyhole—a popular, shallow snorkeling area—but the white sand-pocket lagoon had disappeared, suffocated by southeast swells and buried beneath black oil.

She watched the heavy surf stir up the Witches Brew, spewing the oil halfway up the face of the rusty-colored volcanic cliff. She watched the fierce, black waves pound the rock ledges at the foot of the cliffs, again and again.

Her eyes roamed aimlessly, searching the bottom of the cauldron, until they settled, finally, on the roof of a brown pavilion. The public restrooms? The pavilion was surrounded by flailing palm trees and looked exposed, vulnerable, abandoned.

She felt a pressure in her chest, a shortness of breath, a feeling of disorientation and dizziness.

She yelled—not for help, because she knew it was too late for help, too late to prevent the destruction, too late to save the bay—instead, she yelled out of astonishment and anguish and despair.

Pacing back and forth, she lost her balance and stumbled. Her face struck asphalt; her nose and cheeks smashed against the unyielding, rough surface.

Her cell phone shrilled.

"Hello," she said, mechanically, answering her phone and sitting up.

"How's Hanauma Bay," a man's voice asked.

"It's gone."

"Gone?"

She set the phone down on the asphalt next to her legs, which she had managed to curl beneath her body. The face of the phone was smeared with blood.

The nurse had drawn the white curtains over the wall of windows to keep out the morning sun, although it was cloudy. The room was a typical hospital room, except that all the furnishings were old, including a cheap television mounted on the wall at the foot of the bed. The room smelled of disinfectant.

Keahi watched Toi as she woke up, her face covered in bandages. She was buried beneath white sheets and a beige bedspread, which was tightly tucked. It was a cold, metal-framed bed.

"I dreamed I was back in a hospital bed in Malaysia, in the refugee camp, after the boat trip. And here I am . . . Everything is so wrong, Keahi."

"You never told me about the refugee camp," he said.

"It feels like I was just carried off the boat, but that's impossible, isn't it?" She looked into Keahi's eyes.

"Tell me."

"It was the end of the monsoon season, and we—my Chinese foster parents and I—we had scrimped and saved and traded everything we had for passage." She was silent for a few seconds. "The pirates killed them—my foster parents."

"I was in the hospital for weeks. The sun, the wind, the ocean water, they dehydrated me. I had blisters on my lips and in my mouth. My tongue swelled up. I had tubes in my nose and fluids dripping slowly into my arm through intravenous needles."

"I heard a nurse say that it was a miracle I was alive." Toi recounted the details of the attack. "I jumped into the water so they could not rape me. I remember their laughter. You see, there were sharks. Sharks had been following our small boat for days."

"Oh my God," she said, running her fingers through her black hair, touching the bandages on her cheek and nose and ear. "I must look terrible!" She covered her face with her hands, in embarrassment. "I need to brush my hair. Would you mind if I use the restroom and clean up a bit?"

"No, of course not," Keahi said. "I'll step outside. And I'll let the nurse know that you're awake. I'll come back in a little while, okay?"

"Yes, please come back."

Keahi stood up and walked over to the door. "I'll just have a cup of coffee, then come right back."

"Thank you," she said. Keahi heard a note of relief in her voice.

He stepped into the hallway and pulled the door shut behind him.

They've got to have coffee around here somewhere, he thought. *And a malasada. But where?*

While he was looking for coffee, he met Jack coming down the wide hallway carrying a large bouquet of yellow and white daisies.

"How is she?"

"Much better. She's washing up, so it will be awhile."

"Does she have any family here?"

"No."

"How about Liko?" Liko was Keahi's nephew who lived in a trailer park outside Las Vegas. Liko had spent his last two summer vacations in Hawaii, staying with Keahi.

"No. I haven't called him."

"Why?" Jack asked. "Is he still upset?"

"Upset?"

"About the boy who drowned at Shark's Cove?"

"You knew about that?" Keahi asked. Toi and Keahi had forbidden Liko to dive the lava tubes at Shark's Cove, and then a diver had drowned there, a diver who would have been Liko's dive partner. Upset about the tragedy, Liko had left Oahu before his summer vacation ended.

"Yes," Jack answered. "Liko told me about the argument while he was helping me shingle my roof, before the boy drowned."

"I see," Keahi said. "Hopefully, that's behind us."

Jack's cell phone rang. He read the name on the display and frowned. "I've got to go. Can you give Toi these flowers?"

"Sure," Keahi said, taking the yellow and white bouquet.

He watched Jack walk back down the hall and push the button for the elevator.

Liko hasn't kept in touch, Keahi thought as he watched Jack step into the elevator and turn around. They nodded at each other as the doors closed. *I wonder if he's kept in touch with Toi.*

Later in the day, after Keahi returned to his studio, he was still struggling with whether or not to call Liko.

The nurses had said Toi would be okay. At least there was nothing physically wrong with her. But seeing the marine sanctuary smothered by oil . . . they said Toi would be kept a second night just as a precaution. *Are they concerned about her mental health?* The thought surprised him. He knew how much she loved the ocean and marine life and diving, but still . . . .

Perhaps a call from Liko would help. But he hesitated.

He breathed deeply, hoping it would clear his head, and went out on his lanai. After a few Foster's he began to feel angry at Liko. But why?

And then he suddenly understood: he was angry because Liko had not stayed in touch. At first he had called, but then Liko wasn't one for email or texts.

I'm jealous! He laughed out loud. *And lonely, and I'm hurt. Is my life that vacuous?*

He knew that the important thing was Toi's well-being—her needs, not his personal feelings. She needed help. So he ground his teeth, took a deep breath, and decided to call.

Nevertheless, the BlackBerry weighed a hundred pounds. He tapped in the numbers.

A woman's voice answered.

Surprised, Keahi asked, "Big sister?"

"Who's this?"

"Keahi. I'm calling from Hawaii."

"Ke-ah-hi? That really you?"

Keahi could hear his sister slurring her words. *She's drunk.* He asked, "How are you?"

"Just terrible. You have no idea."

But he did have an idea: a very good idea.

"Is Liko there?"

"Liko? No. He's at the steakhouse, working."

"Please ask him to call me, okay?"

"Shure," she said, but the drunken tone of her voice suggested that she would forget. Then she complained about her trailer, her neighbors, and her personal fate.

Keahi was glad the Pacific Ocean physically separated them. He didn't want such bitterness close by. In fact, he felt himself becoming angry at her.

He allowed her to ramble on for several minutes. After taking the full measure of the current state of her life—and especially Liko's current environment—he quietly said good-bye and hung up.

As he sat on his large hide-a-bed sofa next to the phone, he felt his disappointment towards Liko subside. In its place, now, was a desire to reach out and help the kid. For the first time, Keahi began to imagine what it must be like to be Liko.

He cracked another Foster's.

Keahi's phone rang. He jumped and pounced on it before it finished the second ring. He didn't want it to disturb his neighbors.

"Hello?" He ran his hand over his eyes and tried to clear his sleepy brain.

"Hi, Uncle Keahi." Liko sounded anxious. "I got your message. Is something wrong?"

"Thanks for calling back. There's plenty wrong here. And Toi is in the hospital. She fainted and scraped her face. And she was dehydrated. You know what's going on here, right?" Keahi had thought about what he was going to say to Liko, but he was half asleep, and it was all coming out in a jumble, and it sounded stilted and distant.

"I know about the oil spill, if that's what you mean. But what happened to Toi? Can I talk to her? What hospital is she in? Is she okay?"

"She's doing better. And she wants to hear from you, I know. Here's the number for the hospital." Keahi gave Liko the hospital number and Toi's room number and explained what had happened—he explained about Hanauma Bay— then they both said goodbye, that they would talk more later, and hung up.

Keahi went back to bed and re-ran the conversation in his mind. *He didn't ask how I was doing. But I didn't ask how he was doing, either.*

He tried to get back to sleep, but he fell into a nightmare: he dreamed about overhead cranes hovering next to stacked, twenty-foot long, containers-on-barge, like vultures beside a beast whose belly had been ripped open and entrails exposed. He awoke and sat straight up in bed.

He got up and had a few more Foster's. *To settle my nerves,* he said to himself.

When Liko got home from work, his mother had already passed out on the couch. He watched a little television, and just before the show ended, she woke up. It wasn't until he was getting ready for bed, around midnight, that she remembered Keahi's call.

Liko had picked up the phone immediately and called. Fortunately, Hawaii time was two hours earlier!

But he had to wait until morning before he could call Toi. Now, at ten o'clock Nevada time, Liko punched the hospital number and asked for Toi's room. *It should be about eight Hawaii time*, he thought. He hoped that she was already awake. His stomach felt like someone had been jumping on it. He had almost decided to hang up when a small voice said "Hello?"

"Toi?"

He heard a little cry, then, "Just a minute."

"Toi, are you okay? It's Liko."

The same small voice said, "Yes, I know it's you. Oh, Liko, I'm so glad you called. How did you know—oh, did Keahi call you? Of course, he did." She laughed a little, but it was a nervous, tentative laugh. "I've been a little under the weather, as they say. I guess you know about everything that's been going on here."

Liko wanted so badly to reassure her, to tell her how much he wanted to see her and hold her, but what came out was, "Yeah, Keahi told me. I'm sorry about everything." Liko hated talking on the telephone. It was like his brain abandoned him. He brushed his thick black hair back, paced back and forth with the phone, pleaded with his brain to function just this once, to help him say the right thing and make everything all right for Toi.

He waited for her to talk, feeling uncomfortable. He wondered if his call meant anything to her.

"I have so much to tell you, Liko. I don't even know myself how I feel about . . . about all the destruction here. Did Keahi tell you about the bay?"

He knew she meant Hanauma Bay.

"Yeah, he told me, just briefly. I think I woke him up. He wasn't too talkative." Liko winced at his words, they sounded cold. *Come on brain, damnit!*

Toi laughed a little.

Liko wondered if she missed him. "Toi, I miss you." Then abruptly, "Take care and I'll be thinking about you."

"Bye, Liko. I'm so happy you called. Take care."

Liko replaced the phone, and smiled for the first time in a long time.

During the next two days, Keahi was impressed with the thankless work Masako's volunteers performed. Hundreds signed up. They bagged oiled debris, shoveled oiled gravel, raked oiled sand. Without fanfare they attacked the oil.

In the middle of the fourth day, Keahi stood atop Puu Hawai'iloa on Mokapu Peninsula—Kaneohe Marine Corp Air Station—and gazed out over the coastline of Kaneohe Bay on one side and Kailua Bay on the other. The black oil had filled both bays and had blanketed North Beach; its steep, sandy banks and rocky shoreline were smothered.

The hot air smelled of crude and salt and dampness. It was nauseating. Keahi doubled over and vomited.

As the sun set on the eighth day, thick black oil, like a frothy layer of chocolate mousse, had impacted all 50 miles of beaches on Oahu. Then on the morning of the ninth day it impacted Kauai. Tar bars washed ashore on Niihau on the tenth day. A week later, little black oily turds washed ashore in the Northwestern Hawaiian Islands, too. Tens of thousands of shorebirds died.

CHAPTER
FOUR

When darkness fell the team got together at Ewa Beach to burn a mountain of petroleum-contaminated debris. The special one-time night burn was a reward from Jack to his staff for all the long, eighteen-hour days they had worked during the three weeks since the oil spill. It had required a special open air burning permit, which Kwon deftly handled. He had also called the National Weather Service to check on the wind direction and speed; the winds were blowing away from shore and out to sea.

Masako's volunteers had piled oil-soaked debris 18 feet high on top of two layers of six-mil plastic and a sorbent rug. The volunteers had bermed the pad with an 18-inch high wall of sand. The berm prevented the dripping, viscous black oil from flowing off the plastic and onto the once-white beach.

Pete had hired off-duty police officers to keep the locals off the beach and away from the bonfire—ostensibly to protect them from exposure to the oil and black smoke. Actually, the police were providing privacy.

Now, standing on the beach beneath cloudy skies—neither the moon nor stars were visible—Kwon used a pen-sized flashlight to read his anemometer, which he held at arm's length parallel to his waist. His arthritic hand shook as he read.

"Winds are nine miles per hour," he said.

"Is that good?" Lim asked.

"Yes," Kwon replied. "We need five miles per hour winds to disperse the smoke, to carry it away from shore and out to sea."

"You mean to blow it away from the homes and sleepers," Lim said.

"That's right." Kwon watched the tiny wheel spinning on the anemometer, powered by the wind. "Thank God the trades have returned." He looked to the horizon and saw a bright star twinkle through a momentary gap in the clouds, and he knew that the trade winds were shaking the starlight.

"Toi, the honor is all yours." He handed her a long-stemmed match.

"Me?" She was surprised.

Keahi hoped that it would be cathartic, that she could direct her pain and anger towards the oil-soaked debris and find some relief as fire destroyed it. "We want you to have the honor," he said. "Go ahead. Set the beast on fire."

Toi struck the head of the wooden match against the black strip on the long, oblong matchbox and lit a torch Keahi held for her.

Taking the torch from Keahi with both hands, she stepped over the shallow berm and walked slowly across the slippery plastic pad to the mountain of oil-soaked debris. Standing before the foul-smelling mountain, she worked the head of the torch into a clump of tangled palm fronds soaked in thick black oil.

"Burn, you fucker," she said, so softly Keahi couldn't hear the angst in her voice.

Everyone stood transfixed as tongues of yellow flame climbed up the oil-soaked fronds, like flitting snake tongues tasting the air. Within moments, the entire mountain burst into bright, hot light. Great tongues of orange-yellow flame soared upward.

Keahi stepped forward and put his arm around Toi's shoulders and walked her backwards off the slippery pad. They kept their gaze focused on the beast. Comforting her, he pulled her close to his large frame as the inferno blazed. He felt tiny tremors rippling through her body.

"I tried to call Liko the other day, but I ended up speaking to my sister, his mother. I left a message, and Liko called me back at two in the morning." He chuckled, "Can you believe that? Two in the morning!"

"Thank you, Keahi," Toi said. "He called me, too. And then he called me again after he saw a CNN special report. They showed the destruction of Hanauma Bay. You know, Hanauma Bay was a special place that we shared."

It was a special place for many people, Keahi thought.

"How is your sister?"

He wanted to say: *She's an alcoholic who has wasted away her life in a trailer park in a godforsaken part of the country.* Instead, he said: "The same as usual."

"We've piled up 80,000 tons of this shit," Masako announced, walking up to Keahi and Toi, and gesturing towards the inferno.

Keahi estimated two tons were now ablaze, more or less. He tried to imagine the enormous volume of the remaining debris.

"Plus, we have twice as much oil-saturated booms and absorbent pads," Masako added.

"How do you dispose of booms?" Toi asked, and then sniffled back a runny nose.

"We cut them into three-foot sections, remove all the metal, and then burn them for power."

"What about the oil-contaminated soil?" Kwon asked.

"We've got 200,000 tons of it," Masako replied. "We're trucking it out to Barbers Point and stockpiling it."

"But what are you going to *do* with it?" Kwon insisted.

Keahi observed that Masako was now fidgeting. Being questioned by Kwon annoyed her. *Temper your questions, Kwon*, Keahi thought, *and don't ask anything inappropriate!*

"The Air Force is flying in three thermal treatment units that they tested in the Gulf of Mexico," she said. "And we have contracted for two more."

"What does a thermal treatment unit do?" Kwon asked, pushing another question.

She glared at him and turned to address her answer to Toi. "Once the Air Force sets up the units, we will run contaminated soil through them on conveyor belts. The soil is heated until the petroleum vaporizes. Then the vapors are collected and burned. Dirty soil goes in, sterilized soil comes out."

"Sterilized?" Toi asked.

"Yes, sterilized," Masako replied.

"Then the sand will be dead," Toi stated, in a low voice, as if talking to herself. "All the living organisms in the sand—plants, animals, bacteria, worms, seeds—everything living in the soil will be killed."

"How else can we clean it?" Masako asked. Keahi could hear the exasperation rising in her voice.

"And you're going to put that stuff back on our beaches?" Kwon asked.

Masako turned and glared at him. "Yes. We will put it back on the beaches! What do you want us to do with it?"

Kwon had no reply.

"Listen, you guys," Masako said. "Waikiki is not a natural beach, anyway. It's man-made. When we're done, it will be an improvement. We'll finish with a top dressing of clean, white sand. A good quality sand."

"Probably imported," Kwon retorted.

Masako let his comment pass so there was silence for some seconds.

"Did you hear the governor's speech?" Pete asked, his attention had been focused on the bonfire and he was just now joining the conversation. "He said the beaches will reopen by July 4th. And he said *all*—not just a few."

"Yeah, sure," Lim said, sarcastically. "Let him work 18 hours a day for the next six months!"

Keahi glanced around. Everyone was fatigued.

He looked thoughtfully at Masako. She looked fagged too, though she seemed to thrive on the stress. During the last three weeks, she had kept up a strenuous pace—like everyone else—ignoring her body's need for rest and sleep. Now she looked like she could collapse.

He wondered why she was working so hard. For that matter, he wondered why any of them were working themselves into exhaustion. Not to get the governor re-elected, that was for sure.

"I've finished collecting this week's water column data," Toi said, "so I have a few hours free tomorrow. I can help someone?"

As far as Keahi knew, after Toi's return from the hospital she had done an excellent job catching up on her duties. She had obtained a gallon of virgin product from the tanker and had accumulated extensive water column data that would be used later for fate and transport studies. But he wondered if it was healthy for her to take on additional responsibilities so soon.

When no one asked for her help, she said, "I've never worked so hard in my entire life."

Everyone laughed. It was a common complaint.

"I have a surprise," Masako announced, stepping over to a cooler. She opened the lid and fished in the ice and pulled out an ice-cold Sam Adams. She cracked it and offered it to the closest team member, Pete. "Want a beer?"

"Sure!" Pete said, accepting the amber bottle.

Following his lead, everyone stepped to the cooler, except Kwon.

Masako fished out another Sam Adams, cracked it, took a long swig, and said, "I still can't believe they collided."

"Why not?" Kwon asked. "Cars cross the centerline. Even satellites collide with space junk."

Keahi gave Kwon a disapproving look but was unable to make eye contact because Kwon was too intent on watching for Masako's reaction.

Keahi glanced at Masako. She was piqued.

"Collisions happen." Pete paused just long enough to sip his beer. "Not long ago, two Norwegian tankers collided in the Gulf of Mexico. It could have been catastrophic: one was an ultralarge crude carrier and at the time of the collision, she was carrying a load of Arabian crude oil."

"What happened?" Toi asked.

"She spilled bunker C from her starboard bunker tank. What should have been a routine transfer of oil from one ship to another almost turned into a catastrophe."

They gazed into the inferno and listened to Pete describe other collisions, other disasters.

"How are *you* doing?" Keahi asked Toi, after a pause in the conversation.

"Me? I've got digestive problems: stomachaches, heartburn. My heart races and my palms get sweaty."

"I've got problems, too," Keahi reciprocated. "It takes me longer to fall asleep. In fact, some nights I can't sleep. I just sit on the lanai all night."

"Oh, Keahi," Toi said. She reached out and lightly placed a hand on his forearm.

"Yeah," Lim said. "Me too. I'm more sensitive to noises now. Noises in the neighborhood, things that never used to bother me, now they wake me up." He rubbed his hands together. "It's as if my nerves were hanging outside my body and everything keeps touching them."

"You just drink too much coffee, Lim," Keahi said, trying to lighten the mood.

"I've missed several shots for my rheumatoid arthritis," Kwon volunteered. "Actually, I've missed the last three. Missing the first wasn't too bad. My body hardly noticed it. But since I didn't get the lab work done, I missed the second shot, too. And when I arranged to get the shot at the satellite clinic near my condo, someone forgot to send it. So now it's been three weeks and no shot!"

"I could give you the shot," Keahi said, jokingly.

"Hell," Masako said, leaning close to Keahi so she could whisper, "I'd love to stick a needle in his ass."

Keahi smiled and chugged his beer and dropped the empty bottle into a plastic bag.

"Have another one," Masako said, encouraging him.

"I will, but first I have a surprise." Keahi's face grew solemn. He pulled off his T-shirt, exposing an upper body that could have been cut and polished by Michelangelo. Then, without saying anything further, he started a *hula ki'i*—an ancient dance with stiff movements and postures. As he danced, he chanted a prayer for everyone's health, his voice filling with emotion and cracking like the palm fronds in the fire.

After that, his face broke into a performance smile and he started yet another hula, his graceful body movements imitating Masako's volunteers. He raked oil from the beaches. He skimmed oil from the water. He rubbed oil off the birds. As he danced, he said to Masako, "This hula is something special that I choreographed just for you. I call it '*Hula A'a*,' or 'the dance of the volunteer.'" As he danced around the bonfire he began to chant, telling the story of the Achilles tanker and the ill-fated crew of the longliner and the collision off the coast of Oahu.

On his third trip around the bonfire, the team joined him and tried to imitate his movements: raking oil, skimming oil, rubbing oil off imaginary birds. Afterwards, they laughed and applauded each other's efforts, and Toi hugged Keahi, and Masako handed him another Sam Adams, and Pete backslapped him affectionately.

The team, now relaxed, grew quiet, stared at the bonfire. A few tired heads began to nod.

Finally, Lim ventured: "I've got some news."

"Let me guess," Kwon said. "You're going to jump ship and move to the mainland?"

Everyone laughed.

"Well, no, but don't think that I haven't been looking for a mainland job." Lim waited a moment, hoping to build suspense, and then he said, "Isn't anyone going to ask me, 'What's your big news?'"

"Okay," Toi said, playing along, "What's your big news?"

"I'm going to be a father!"

"Congratulations!" Toi said, genuinely happy for him.

"And I want to invite all of you to celebrate."

"When is the baby due?" Toi asked.

"July."

"Your wife must be happy."

"Yes," Lim said. "She is very happy."

Everyone accepted his invitation to lunch.

Keahi, however, turned his attention back to the inferno. *What a time to have a baby*, he thought. Nevertheless, he felt jealous, and that surprised him.

PART TWO
TEAM TOGETHERNESS

CHAPTER FIVE

IT WAS THE FIRST WEEK OF FEBRUARY when the team members got together to celebrate Lim's impending fatherhood. They met at a Chinese restaurant known for excellent dim sum. Everyone had jumped at the opportunity to get together; being together as a group gave them a collective feeling of comfort.

Now, sitting in a white wicker chair at a large table at the back of the restaurant, surrounded by his teammates, Keahi observed that the dining area was almost empty. Besides the team, only one couple was having lunch.

"The tourists are still missing."

"Yeah," Lim responded, "tourism is hemorrhaging." He pushed back his chair and stood up. "Please excuse me." Keahi watched him walk through the quiet restaurant and disappear down a silent hallway to the men's room. The near-empty restaurant was depressing.

Kwon, however, was in a jubilant mood. He was devouring a yellow chicken foot, gnawing its rubbery pad, sucking its gelatinized toes. Licking his fingers, he discarded a few small bones onto a plate in the center of the table. Then he reached into a large bowl of black beans and picked out another foot.

"How's the *sui mai*?" Keahi asked.

"*Ono.*"

Kwon sucked off the black bean sauce. "Do you guys really think the world needs another kid?" He pulled the foot out of his mouth and pointed it in Masako's direction. "I mean, look at China, the population has already grown to a billion."

The timing of the question appalled Keahi, but fortunately Lim was in the restroom.

"Rationally it doesn't make a lot of sense," Kwon said, "but I am happy for Lim."

"Well, then," Keahi said, "I propose a toast to Norman Borlaug."

"Who's he?" Toi asked.

"Norman Borlaug? He bred dwarf wheat in Mexico, and then taught Pakistani farmers how to grow it. That's what prevented mass starvation in the 60s and 70s."

"To the end of hunger," Toi proposed.

Everyone raised and clinked their glasses together, even Kwon. But he quipped, "Babies are parasites."

"What?" Toi said. "You don't mean that."

"Oh yes I do. Just think about it. First, this egg, this foreign body, develops into a hollow, circular ball and attaches itself to some part of your uterine wall. Then it secretes an enzyme and attacks the lining of your uterus."

"Get out," Toi said, her eyebrows narrowed into a grimace.

"It does," Kwon said. "I swear. That's what happens. The fertilized egg digests a big hole in the uterus, so it will have a place to bury itself while it grows. Then it taps into the host blood supply. For a long time it feeds off small blood vessels and capillaries, like a vampire."

Everyone had stopped eating.

"And it gets worse. It sends out projections like tiny hoses to anchor itself and to suck nourishment from your body. Later it grows an umbilical cord—this big, thick cord whose sole purpose is to suck nutrients and then deposit wastes into your body. And after a week has passed, it has built itself a cozy little nest, right inside of you."

Keahi thought about that. "So the fetus has found a way to hide itself so the mother's body doesn't attack and destroy it? Amazing."

Kwon looked up and down the table. Everyone was staring at him.

"Jesus Christ!" Masako said. "That's the most perverted, warped thing I've ever heard."

"Well," Kwon said, "I'm just stating the facts." He flashed a smile, raising his eyebrows high.

Masako pushed herself back from the table and frowned at him.

Keahi noted the underlying tension and sadness behind Kwon's words and he guessed that he didn't really consider babies to be parasites or vampires or aliens. So what was his problem? Why was he behaving so badly? What was his motivation?

As Keahi struggled to understand Kwon's motives, Lim returned from the restroom. Before he sat down, though, he noticed the expressions on everyone's faces.

"What? What did I miss? What happened?"

"Does anyone want some dessert?" the waitress asked.

"No thanks!" everyone said, almost in unison.

Lim looked at everyone, suspiciously.

"Kwon was telling us his version of the stork," Masako said.

"And?" Lim asked.

"Believe me, you don't want to know."

Lim pursed his lips.

"Hey, I wish your wife was here," Toi said, changing the subject. "How is she?"

"Yeah, please give her our congratulations," Keahi said.

Suddenly embarrassed, Lim apologized for her absence. In fact, he over-apologized, and then he invited everyone to celebrate the Chinese New Year with him and to meet his wife, Limen. "We can start the celebration with the Lion Dances in Chinatown. It's the Year of the Dog."

"I'd like that," Keahi said, quickly.

Lim and Limen, he thought. *Like lemon and lime.* He set his empty wine glass on the table in front of him and the waiter immediately filled it. *Lemon, lime and little kumquat. Would anyone name their child Kumquat?* He leaned forward and picked up his wine glass. *I've drunk too much*, he thought. The plum wine was sweet and easy to drink. *Or was Limen a nickname*? Deciding to slow down on the wine, he took a small sip, and then set his glass on the table. *I'll pound down some Foster's when I get home.*

CHAPTER SIX

LIM AND HIS WIFE LIMEN STOOD AT THE CURB in Chinatown next to Keahi, talking with Toi. Limen held a small umbrella which was bright yellow, red, and green like the lion dancers, who were working their way slowly, very slowly down the street. It was a monotonously slow parade.

Keahi and Kwon were discussing the voracious appetite of the lion; parade-goers were feeding paper currency into its mouth as it meandered down the dirty street.

"They do that for good luck," Keahi said.

"Then they're throwing their money away," Kwon concluded, emphatically.

Masako and her boyfriend, who had introduced himself as a bouncer at a ritzy Korean nightclub, were seated in folding chairs in front of Kwon and Keahi, and they were holding hands. The bouncer was also of Japanese ancestry.

The team wanted to sit down next to them on the curb—their legs were tired from standing—but there was trash in the gutter and further down the sidewalk they had stepped around vomit. Drunks slept on these concrete sidewalks and sometimes had a rough night of it.

To Keahi, Chinatown was a filthy place. He never enjoyed coming down here and he seldom did, but today he had made an exception because Lim had invited him and he had wanted to meet Limen.

At the moment, though, she was talking with Toi.

"How are you and the baby?" Toi asked.

"Oh, we're fine," Limen replied, in a strong Chinese accent. She rested her hand on her extended stomach. "How are *you*?"

"Me? I'm getting by."

"Honey," Limen said, a note of concern in her voice, "Lim told me about Hanauma Bay—how special it was to you. I'm so sorry."

Toi thought a moment. "This may sound silly, but on some level I'm still trying to make sense of it all."

"We're all trying to make sense of this mess, honey. No one was prepared for this. No one imagined how bad it was going to be."

That was the second time that Limen had called Toi 'honey.' It sounded weird to Keahi, kind of shocking, kind of funny.

"I've had nightmares," Toi said. "They always start the same: I'm snorkeling at Hanauma Bay, surrounded by colorful fish, and I'm happy, but then darkness envelops me, slowly. It gets darker and darker and becomes harder and harder to breathe, like there is a pressure inside my chest, like my organs are collapsing. Then I wake up in a panic."

"Oh, honey," Limen said, looking into Toi's eyes, "that sounds awful." She shifted her brightly colored umbrella to her left hand and put her arm around Toi and gave her a hug. "You're going to be okay. Look how bright the sun is. Feel how warm it is."

"Believe me, honey," Limen said, hugging Toi again, and patting her gently on the shoulder, "right now you have nothing to be afraid of."

At that moment, Keahi turned his attention from Limen and Toi to Kwon. Kwon was standing directly behind Masako and her boyfriend, who were seated in hot pink and baby blue folding chairs.

"What club do you work at?" Kwon asked the bouncer.

The bouncer looked over his shoulder at Kwon and replied, "Club Femme Star. Been there?"

"No," Kwon said.

"You should stop by. See the show." The bouncer affectionately punched Masako's shoulder and gave her a smile. "This girl can pole dance."

"You're a stripper?" Kwon asked Masako. His voice went flat.

"She's one of the best."

Masako elbowed the bouncer.

"Sorry," he said. "I mean *the* best. She's the best."

Kwon's face instantly showed disapproval.

"Yes, Kwon, it's for the money," Masako said. "Don't look so shocked. I can't keep up my lifestyle working on a state salary. What business is it of yours anyway?"

It made sense to Keahi: Masako liked nice clothes, drove a BMW convertible, and lived in an expensive condominium at Harbor Court—she had the best of everything. Besides, he thought, surveying her seated body in her hot pink chair, the pole dancing seemed to be keeping her trim and fit. If done gymnastically, he thought, pole dancing was a great aerobic workout.

A sadness filled Kwon's face.

The bouncer said to him, "Your oil spill's good for business."

"*My—*"

Firecrackers landed in the street, directly in front of their group. The large packet flashed and exploded and landed at Masako's feet. She screamed and sat frozen with her hands making fists on her knees.

Kwon's arthritic body seemed to implode upon itself, as he flinched.

The bouncer, however, jumped up and kicked the firecrackers back into the middle of the street.

Shredded firecracker paper—gray and black and red – floated in front them. As if in slow motion, the paper appeared to hang motionless in the air for several seconds, and then slowly dropped to the ground.

"God!" Masako yelled, holding her hands over her ears.

The smell of burnt powder mingled with the smell of greasy sidewalks and the smell of urine.

And then the dragon stopped yet again while a group of kids fed it more dollars, one at a time. The team waited, bored.

Keahi felt uncomfortable. He shifted his feet. He wiped his forehead and neck, and then wiped his palms on his tan khakis, temporarily staining them dark.

After a while, the bouncer turned sideways in his chair to scan the group, which put him at eye level with Kwon's legs. "What happened to your legs, brah? Shark attack or what?"

"Shark?" Kwon repeated. "No, just an accident."

"Look like da kine, drop in one wood chip'ah," the bouncer said. "You should wear jeans, brah. Cover your legs."

How rude, Keahi thought.

Kwon became silent, his face pasty white. After the dragon passed, which took a long time, he turned around and started pushing his way through the crowd that had formed behind him.

"Wait for me," Keahi called after him.

"The parade's too slow," Kwon answered. "I'm going to explore the stores."

Keahi looked up and down the block. There was a small shop, a couple of bars and crowds of people. They had been standing in front of a Chinese food market.

"Okay if I tag along?"

"Suit yourself."

Trailing behind Kwon as he pushed his way through the mostly Chinese-American crowd, Keahi noted that Kwon now walked stiffly, favoring his left leg.

Keahi weaved through the crowd and caught up with him. "I heard what the bouncer said."

When Kwon didn't say anything, Keahi added, "I'm sorry that I didn't prevent the accident."

"It wasn't your fault," Kwon said. "The wind blew, the door slammed and the aquarium shattered. It wasn't any-one's fault."

No, it WAS my fault. It was my responsibility to ensure that the site was secure before you entered. Keahi cleared his throat. "I hope that you will accept my apology. Please forgive me for the pain and the suffering that I have caused you."

"Keahi, I know what happened. It was an accident. I don't blame you. And I certainly don't hold you responsible."

"I'd feel much better if you would accept my apology."

Kwon stopped and stared at Keahi. "If it will make you feel better, your apology is accepted. I forgive you."

"Thanks, that means a lot to me."

Kwon smiled. "Well, I hope you can sleep better now." Then he added, "I do have a really bad headache, though. Help me find something for my headache, okay?"

"Sure," Keahi said.

They started walking again and picked up their pace.

In the next block they came to an apothecary store; the sign on the window indicated that they spoke English and Chinese. Kwon pulled the door open and held it for Keahi to pass through. Once inside they stopped at the front counter and waited for the salesman, who they could see at the back of the long, narrow store, busy at the top of a ladder.

"Can you believe that Masako invited a bouncer?" Kwon asked resentfully.

"He's just a temporary entertainment, one of many boyfriends."

"One of many?"

"That's the impression I get," Keahi said. "I sense that she has never been lucky in love."

"Lucky?"

"I think she goes through boyfriends the way you eat plate lunches."

"So this guy isn't anyone special?"

"A bouncer at a nightclub? I doubt it. Besides, I doubt that she makes commitments."

The lanky man climbed down the ladder and walked over to where Kwon and Keahi were standing. "Can I help you?" he asked, speaking excellent English without any Chinese accent. Despite his obvious Chinese ancestry, he had piercing blue gray eyes behind epicanthic eyelids. He focused on Kwon, studying him. "'Tis love, 'tis love. I have a most excellent love potion."

"Love potion?" Kwon repeated, taken aback. "No thanks! However, I do need something for my legs. Do you have something that will change them? Make them normal again?"

Keahi knew that Kwon was joking. He wondered how the old salesman would react.

The man leaned across the glass counter and looked down at the scars on Kwon's legs. "Physical metamorphosis?" A fold of loose skin under his chin wattled as he laughed. "Nope. I don't do physical metamorphosis."

"How about headaches?" Kwon asked.

"Sure! Headaches I cure." The old man directed them to the opposite side of his store and selected a remedy from a large display case of natural medicines.

When the old man gave Kwon the remedy, they walked over to an old-style register where the old man counted out Kwon's change into his upturned hand. Along with the change, into Kwon's palm he placed a second packet.

"It's a love potion," he said. "Very powerful."

"Give me a break," Kwon said. Nevertheless, he gazed with wonder at the small packet.

Keahi chuckled, which caused Kwon to blush.

"Mix it with an alcoholic drink," the old man instructed.

"Do I take it or do I give it to her?"

"Ah! That is the challenge. You must take it *together*. And at the same time!"

"So they must share the same drink," Keahi asked.

"That would work," the old man said.

Kwon stuffed the packet into his shirt pocket with the headache cure. He thanked the old man and tipped him five dollars.

They walked half a block down the street before Kwon stopped in front of a trash can. Reaching into his shirt pocket, he withdrew both packets. "No telling what's in this shit," he said, dropping one into the open-topped trashcan.

"Wise decision," Keahi said.

"If you see a Long's drugstore or even an ABC Store, please tell me—I do need something for this throbbing headache."

"What? You kept the love potion?"

"I'm not *lolo*—crazy—you know. What if this stuff actually works?" Kwon smiled broadly, then groaned and rubbed his right temple. He dropped the packet containing the love potion back into his shirt pocket.

"Well, who's the girl?"

"Who do you think?"

"No way!" Keahi said. Masako was the only girl that Kwon had shown an interest in, and that interest was not a healthy one. "You're kidding, right?"

Kwon's face suddenly showed his pain. "Listen, I'm going to walk around for a while. I'll rejoin you guys later." Then he abruptly said farewell and walked off down the block, alone. After a few yards he gave a dismissive farewell wave with his hand raised high in the air, without turning around or looking back.

Keahi turned around and started back to rejoin his teammates. As he walked alone in the crowd, he thought about what Kwon had just told him. No way! The idea of Kwon and Masako, as a couple, was so farfetched that Keahi gave it no further consideration other than to dismiss it as a bad joke. *I'm sorry guy. I'm really sorry. I know that you need a painkiller. But I know that it's for your legs, not for your head, and certainly not for your heart.*

Kwon didn't rejoin his teammates before the parade ended, so he wasn't there when Lim and Limen invited everyone to join them the next day for an additional day of celebration, including the crowning of the Narcissus Queen, lantern parades, and dancing in the streets. They all declined, however, because they were dead tired, and for the most part they felt miserable.

That afternoon, as they walked back to the parking garage on Hotel Street, Lim told Keahi he was actively looking for a job on the mainland and he planned to bail out as soon as he had an opportunity. "I don't want to spend the next five years cleaning up someone else's mess. Everything here has gone to hell. We've made up our mind, Limen and I. We're leaving as soon as I find another job."

As they walked the last block to the garage, Keahi chatted with Masako and appraised the bouncer. The oil spill had energized her. Keahi thought, *Except for her choice in men she is really shining. She knows how to work with people. She's a superb coordinator.*

The bouncer was handsome and suntanned, and appeared affable with a quick smile, a joke, and an extremely loud laugh. He made a good first impression. Nevertheless, experience allowed Keahi to recognize the bouncer's underlying personality: he was ugly and self-centered and mean, mentally and physically abusive to anyone that he perceived as weaker or at a disadvantage. Wasn't that the way he behaved towards Kwon? Abusive? But worse of all, Keahi guessed that the bouncer's skewed values would enable him to interpret right and wrong as little more than what was best for him in any given situation. *A rotten personality.*

Later, as he was driving back to his studio apartment, Keahi reflected on his own situation. Like Masako, he was giving more than one hundred percent of himself to the cleanup. Why? Was it because he liked being part of a larger effort? Perhaps. But what else could he do? He wasn't allowed to work the child care facility explosion. That was now Santos's case.

Sleepless nights, however, were something he now shared with Toi. And Keahi suspected that Kwon's arthritis and aching legs kept him awake, too. Everyone was suffering from sleep deprivation. Except perhaps Pete. Why had Pete declined Lim's invitation to watch the parade? It wasn't that he was antisocial. In fact, he was very amiable, downright gregarious most of the time. And as far as Keahi knew, Pete liked Lim. *He probably spent the day hiking*, Keahi guessed. *He loves hiking and surfing almost as much as he loves his work. One lucky guy.*

CHAPTER SEVEN

The waitress greeted Masako and the team in the waiting area of the upscale sushi restaurant. She bowed deeply, then led them to a private dining room.

Before entering, Masako slipped out of her medium-heeled black dress shoes and pushed them against the wall, next to the doorway, ready for her to slip back into when the meal was over and it was time to leave. Following her lead, the team removed their shoes, too, lining them up against the wall.

After entering, Masako instructed everyone where to sit around the low, rectangular table. Then she sat down on the floor with her thighs together and her stocking feet tucked under her butt, settling comfortably into a mermaid position despite wearing a mid-thigh-length chiffon ruffled red dress. Everyone followed her example and took their designated places on the floor.

Toi, wearing jeans, sat cross-legged like the guys, and Masako corrected her, insisting that she also sit mermaid style. "You must keep your knees below the top of the table," Masako admonished.

Obediently, Toi repositioned herself on her pillow.

Lim was corrected next. "Please, don't wipe your face with the *oshibori!*" Masako frowned at him. "It is for your hands, not your face!"

Lim tossed the *oshibori* onto the table, nonchalantly.

Flustered, Masako raised her voice to the waitress, "*Betsu-betsu ni onegaishimasu.*"

The young waitress who was handing out menus nodded acknowledgement.

Everyone looked at Masako for her to explain.

"I told her you are a band of barbarians."

Another girl entered and collected the *oshibori* in a covered basket, including the one that Lim had tossed unsociably onto the table, and then she left the room. All the employees were Japanese-American, Keahi noted. And the room was traditional Japanese, too, right down to the traditional colors of red and cream and black and white: white walls; opaque, cream-colored, screens; black wainscoting and furniture; and, of course, Masako dressed in red. Keahi leaned forward and rested the sides of his wrists on the gold trim that edged the black, lacquered table. The low-to-the-ground table was not suited for his large, muscular frame.

The team ordered. When their food arrived, Masako picked up her chopsticks—the long, Japanese kind with pointed ends—and said, "*Itakakimasu, bon appetit.*"

Kwon saluted her with his chopsticks. He poured a red sauce over his bowl of white rice and stirred. Then he greedily shoveled the mixture from the side of the bowl into his mouth. When his mouth was stuffed, he set his half-empty bowl down and became interested in the appetizers, which included a plate of tempura- mushrooms. "Fresh shiitake!" he exclaimed, spewing rice in all directions.

Keahi watched Masako watching Kwon as he attacked the serving bowl of mushrooms. He speared a large, fluffy, deep-fried *shiitake* with his chopsticks and began nibbling the mushroom around the edges, as he passed the bowl to Toi. Masako's expression conveyed both disgust and regrets.

Regrets for what? Keahi wondered, as he shifted his aching buttocks on his pillow.

He glanced at Pete. Pete had been so busy eating that he hadn't said anything.

I wonder if he is disappointed in me, Keahi thought. *I just don't share his passion for the work.*

At that moment Pete looked up and they made eye contact and exchanged smiles.

"This was a good choice, Masako," Pete said. After the success of their Chinatown outing, the team had decided that they would take turns choosing restaurants.

"A very good choice," Keahi added.

Masako smiled, accepting the compliments.

In the meantime, Kwon had finished the skewered mushroom, and was now sucking yellow-brown batter off the end of his chopsticks. "*Ono!*"

"Yes, they are delicious," Toi agreed, tasting one of the mushrooms.

"In Japan, they sell shiitake sprouts in the spring and fall," Masako told Toi, making an effort to ignore Kwon. "They're grown in the shade, on chestnut logs. You make shallow cuts in the logs and then sprinkle them with spawn."

"Ever go mushroom hunting?" Toi asked.

"Sure," Masako replied, "when I was a kid. We hunted for *matsutake*—pine mushrooms—in the red pine forests around Kyoto."

"Weren't you afraid of the poisonous ones?"

"Nah, pine mushrooms are easy to identify. Their caps grow very large, wider than your hand. And they are easy to find. We prized the half-opened ones. My aunt used them in *matsutake-meshi,* rice cooked with pine mushroom. Now *that* was *ono!*"

They exchanged more pleasant memories until Toi abruptly excused herself and hurried to the ladies' room.

When more than ten minutes had passed and she hadn't returned, Keahi became concerned and asked Masako to check on her. Masako obliged, but without any earnestness.

They didn't return until much later in the meal. Toi's eyes were puffy and Masako was uncomfortably quiet.

"Is everything okay?" Keahi asked, putting down his chopsticks.

"Everything's fine," Masako said, the tone of her voice making it clear that he should drop his inquiry. "No problem."

Yeah, right, Keahi thought.

In their absence, Keahi, Lim and Kwon had gorged on plate after plate of sushi until they were stuffed, the waitress delivering plates as ordered, including one called 'warrior roll,' in honor of the University of Hawaii's football team. It came wrapped in foil and was set aflame at the table.

When the checks came, Keahi paid the whale's share.

Keahi held the silver-colored microphone in his hand and it felt marvelous! Encouraged by Toi, he had taken the stage at the karaoke bar, which was only a short walk down the street from the Japanese restaurant. Performing was his very essence.

He was halfway through his second song when he saw Toi jump up from her seat and go directly to the restroom, quickly, just like she had in the restaurant. This time, however, Masako followed close behind.

Later, as he was finishing his third song, Masako returned to their table at the back of the bar, but without Toi.

Concerned, his heart went out of the lyrics and his voice trailed off and, unconsciously, he imparted a melancholy feeling to what should have been a happy ending. The unintended affect impressed the crowd, however, and they enthusiastically applauded.

Surprised, Keahi bowed and passed the microphone to the next karaoke singer, who stepped up to the stage, also encouraged by friends. Keahi then returned to the table.

"I'm in awe," Pete said, filling Keahi's sake cup as Masako sat down. "Your voice is incredible."

"*Kanpai!*" Keahi said, quickly swallowing the cup of sake, which was immediately refilled. The small cup seemed tiny compared to his big hands and massive, muscular forearms.

"Amazing!" Kwon said.

"Thank you."

"*Kanpai!*" they all said in unison and emptied their cups.

"Why haven't you done anything?" Masako asked.

"Like what?"

"Well, if I had your voice I wouldn't be working for the government."

He raised his right eyebrow and threw Masako a questioning look. Then he asked, "Is Toi okay?"

Masako hesitated, then answered, "She's having anxiety attacks."

"Why? What's going on?"

"The oil spill." Masako frowned. "Where have you been the last three months?"

At the mention of the oil spill, it was as if an uninvited intruder had suddenly entered the bar and taken a seat at their table. Kwon, Lim, Pete and Keahi looked down at the tabletop, each staring at a small area directly in front of them.

"Hell!" Masako exclaimed, "I even thought I was pregnant! Can you believe that? Me? Pregnant?"

The guys stared harder at the surface of the table.

"My period stopped," Masako explained, attacking their modesty. "Can you believe it?"

"Huh?" Kwon said, suddenly looking up, shocked. "Did I miss something? What does pregnancy and 'that time of the month' have to do with Toi? Is she pregnant?"

"It's the damned oil spill!" She didn't call Kwon an idiot but it was implied by the inflection in her voice.

They were now all staring at Masako. In fact, everyone in the bar followed her loud voice, and glanced at her.

"She's having stomach cramps. She says her heart flutters, her feet and hands go numb and get tingly, her fingers grow cold. Sometimes she's nauseated."

"So what does that mean?" Keahi asked, concerned.

Masako seemed edgy, as if she had more to tell but was holding something back.

Reacting to his persistent gaze, Masako stated, "I can't get involved, not right now. I just can't get involved."

"Can I help?" Keahi asked.

Masako shrugged.

The team was on foot, walking through Waikiki to another bar. When they arrived at where Pete was parked along the street, Pete said, "I'm calling it a night. I have to meet the navy response team tomorrow at Pearl Harbor, so I need to get some rest."

"But tomorrow's Saturday," Keahi said.

"I know," Pete said. "But I need to get some things done. Would you like to join me?"

"Heaven's no!"

"See you Monday," someone added.

Pete drove away and the team continued their walk.

Toi, walking beside Masako, had her hand on her stomach. "How are the volunteers?" she asked Masako.

"Still working hard."

"How do you keep them motivated? You'd think they'd be burnt out."

"They are. Their work is *monotonous*—the same thing over and over and over again—picking up oil-contaminated debris, raking miles and miles of oil-soaked sand, removing tar balls, skimming oil by hand. It is boring work. Insanely boring."

"It's the contractors who are getting bitchy," Lim said over his shoulder. He was leading the team, walking immediately in front of Masako and Toi. Keahi and Kwon were bringing up the rear. "One yelled at me today."

Masako nodded agreement.

"You still plan to leave Hawaii?" Toi asked him.

"Good God, yes! Hawaii may recover, but it's going to take a long, long time. Tourism is down what, 95 percent? Travel-related businesses are going bankrupt. My friends are losing their jobs. Waikiki is a ghost town. No, *Hawaii* is a ghost state. Limen and I have decided to move to Vancouver."

"How about you, Kwon?" Toi asked, taken aback by Lim's reply. "Are you staying?"

"Except for the red tape, I enjoy my work," Kwon said. Kwon had been unusually quiet throughout the evening. "It has a certain novelty. So, yes, I'm staying."

"And you, Keahi?" Toi asked.

"Hell," Keahi answered, chuckling, "I'd rather spend the day bench pressing 300 pounds than working with you guys."

They all laughed, but without much humor.

The group stopped at a bar, and when Masako went to order a round of Kirin, Keahi poked Kwon in the ribs and pointed out a young Japanese man who was flirting with

Masako. She appeared flattered that the young man was interested in her. Her eyes opened wide as she talked to him.

"From the way he's dressed, the Armani trousers, the Gucci shoes, the gold watch and that heavy gold necklace, I'd say he's rich." Keahi paused. "Definitely wealthy. And handsome." Keahi admired his strong jaw and distinctive cheekbones.

Kwon didn't offer a comment, but his expression disapproved of the man. When Masako brought her young admirer back to the table and introduced him to Toi and the other guys, saying "Meet Samy," Kwon was clearly unhappy, his brow deeply furrowed.

Masako leaned back in her chair, one hand playing with her hair, the other hand caressing her bare knee. She was smiling at Samy.

Samy started a conversation with her in Japanese.

"I'm sorry," Kwon interrupted. "I didn't catch that."

Masako frowned.

"*Hashigo*," Samy explained. He smiled and his teeth were bright white. "You are bar hopping and you are on your third binge or '*sanjikai*.'"

"We don't speak Japanese," Kwon said, enclosing Keahi, Lim, and Toi with a wave of his hand. "It's rude to sit at someone's table and then not include them in the conversation. Don't you think so?"

"My apology," Samy said. "You know, if you were in Japan, everyone would want to talk to you, to practice their English."

"But we're not in Japan," Kwon said, pointedly. "We are in an American bar in Hawaii. And we speak English here, not Japanese."

Samy smiled—a condescending smile—as if he was laughing at Kwon.

"Are you on vacation?" Masako asked.

"Yes," Samy replied. "You could say I'm on vacation."

"You could say?" Kwon asked. "What does that mean, 'you could say?' Are you on vacation or not?"

"Well, for me, every day is a vacation."

"That makes no sense," Kwon said.

"Ah, but I don't work," Samy said.

"Everyone works," Kwon countered.

"Not me," Samy said. "My father left me a substantial annuity. I'm 28 and I haven't worked since my 21st birthday." He smiled again.

The smile reminded Keahi of the local politicians who stood on the street corners preceding reelection, waving campaign signs, advertising little more than their names in bold letters. They waved 'shaka' and smiled at all the passing cars, indiscriminately.

"What did you do before you inherited this fortune?" Kwon asked.

"I was a professional student."

"What did you study?"

"Everything and nothing. I had three hundred semester hours. My father used to say, 'Samy, someday Todai will make a mistake and graduate you, accidentally.'"

"You have *never* worked?" Toi asked, disbelief in her voice.

"Well, for a while I worked as a paralegal temp. Nothing permanent, just temporary assignments. It was interesting. And of course I had the choice of whether I accepted an assignment or not."

"Of course," Keahi said, feigning a smile. Then he turned to his teammates and said, "Please excuse me. I'll be back in a minute." He got up and found his way through the busy bar to the men's room.

Standing in front of the urinal, he sighed, deeply, loudly. "God, I've pissed my life away!" Embarrassed, he quickly looked over his shoulder to see if anyone had heard his outburst. He was relieved to find that he was alone.

I should be living free and independent, not that idiot Samy who is wasting his life doing nothing. I should have followed my dreams. I should have pursued my music, my singing. He thought about how much he had enjoyed performing at the karaoke bar earlier in the evening. *I should be living the life of an artist. Instead, I'm a bureaucrat.*

"Damn!" he said aloud. "God, I'd give anything to have another opportunity." His voice echoed dully off the bathroom walls. He tucked and zipped, then kicked the wall to the right of the urinal. Then he returned to the table.

Samy was talking. "And there I was, alone with this big guy, and he was wearing nothing but flowery tattoos."

Everyone burst out laughing.

Keahi knew that he had missed a joke. Flowery tattoos? Was it an anti-gay joke? He looked sullenly at his teammates. Surely they wouldn't have laughed at an anti-gay joke, would they?

"I love Hawaii!" Samy exclaimed.

"Why is that?" Kwon asked, his voice edgy.

"I can loaf here and not feel ashamed or pressured to do anything. Here, it's wonderful. No one expects me to do anything. I can sleep until nine and then lie in bed and daydream until ten, order room service and have a late breakfast with champagne and orange juice, then take a long hot shower and go to the pool for an afternoon swim. It's wonderful! I could live here forever. And they wait on me hand and foot. What is the expression you use? Aloha? Yes, much aloha here."

"Doesn't it get boring?" Toi asked.

"Boring? No. Lonely? Yes." He took hold of Masako's hand. "The week after the spill, everyone disappeared! I thought I was the only tourist left! It was like the rapture, except Jesus called all the tourists to heaven." He laughed.

"How terrible for you," Kwon mumbled.

"No, but—" Samy lowered his voice and said, "It wouldn't be so bad, except for the military guys."

"Military guys?" Kwon asked without lowering his voice.

"Because the beaches are oiled, all the—" Samy looked around him and lowered his voice to a whisper, "all the military guys have no place to go but the bars. It's terrible! Every bar you go to, military guys!"

Keahi surveyed the room. Yes, there were a lot of military guys in the bar, which Keahi hadn't noticed until now. In normal times he would have been aware of everything in his environment: the colors, the smells, the décor, how people were dressed. But now he seemed to zone in and out.

Kwon ordered another gin and tonic for himself and another round of drinks for the team, including another Moscow Mule for Masako, her second in the last hour.

An hour later, after yet another Moscow Mule, Masako was feeling very talkative—so talkative, in fact, that she shared a painful childhood memory. She told the story of her father visiting her in Japan during *hanami*, the time of cherry blossom viewing.

"I was so excited," Masako said. "My father was coming to visit me. And my aunt said he had bought me a pair of new roller skates. When he arrived, he took me to Ueno Park—that's in Tokyo."

She described the rows and rows of pinkish-white blossoms on the cherry trees.

"He had this big brown box. I knew the roller skates were inside that box. I knew it. I was so happy!" She sipped her Moscow Mule, holding it in both hands.

"I wanted to skate for him. I wanted to make him happy." She tilted her glass and looked into the top of her drink. "You see, my mother was a beautiful skater." She looked at her drink again and then looked up.

"He helped me put on the skates." She looked at Toi.

"And then I tried...." Her voice went flat. "You see, my mother, when she skated, she made it look so easy...."

"I felt so ashamed. I wanted to skate for him. But how could I? I had never worn skates before." Masako drank the rest of the Moscow Mule and shook her head from side to side.

"Instead of comforting me, he scolded me."

Keahi noticed that Kwon was engrossed with her story, hanging on every word.

"When I fell . . . he got angry."

"Why?" Toi asked. "Why would he get angry?"

"Because my mother had died the previous year," Masako said. "That's why he sent me away . . . to live in Japan with my aunt." Masako stared into her empty glass. "He needed my mother, not me." Her head bobbed up and down. "I remember he turned his face from me and cried." She looked up from her empty glass. "And that is when I realized that we are all alone in the world."

"That's so sad," Toi said.

"I remember that it rained. It was a cold rain. And the cherry blossoms fell with the rain."

"You are an only child?" Samy asked.

"No," Masako replied. "I have a younger brother. He's still in Japan."

"Your father is a successful businessman?" Samy asked.

"Very successful," Masako replied. "My father does packaged weddings. He owns two wedding chapels, one on Oahu and one on Maui. And he has plans to build a third on Kauai."

"Do you work for your father?" Samy asked.

"Me?" Masako asked. "Weddings?"

They all laughed, even Kwon.

An hour later, Kwon became violently ill. He complained that his temples were pounding and that he was nauseated.

At first Keahi thought he was drunk; however, he was not slurring his words and he was still able to follow and add to the team's conversation, lucidly.

Masako, on the other hand, was merciless. She *was* drunk. And she chided Kwon for being unable to handle his liquor.

That angered Kwon and his condition grew worse.

"Keahi, I need to go home," he begged, suddenly frantic, barely holding himself together. "Can you take me?"

"Sure."

A few minutes later, seated in Keahi's car, he was pressing his palms against the sides of his head, just above his ears, vigorously massaging his temples, as the car bounced through one pothole after another.

"Do you have to hit every pothole?"

"What?"

"Every damned pothole. Do you have to hit every pothole?"

After Keahi drove a few blocks, Kwon yelled, "Pull over!" His face was pale.

Keahi pulled over to the curb, and Kwon threw open the passenger door and vomited into the gutter. Then he climbed into the backseat and laid down, moaning and rolling on the narrow seat.

Keahi drove on to Kwon's condominium complex and parked on the street.

When the car stopped, Kwon tried to sit up but the nausea forced him to immediately lie back down.

Keahi patiently waited.

Long minutes passed until Kwon was able to sit up, and again until he decided to make his way out of the car. After a few steps, though, he collapsed.

Keahi had to pick him up in his arms, as one would a small child, and carry him to the entrance of the building. "I need your keys."

Kwon fished in his pants pocket. Nickels and pennies fell to the clay-tiled floor and rolled away, noisily. Finally, he pulled out his keys and dropped them into Keahi's shirt pocket. He had his arms around Keahi's neck, although it wasn't necessary.

When they reached the entrance, Keahi set him on his feet, leaning him against the light brown, painted concrete wall of the entryway. Holding him in place with one hand, he took the keys from his shirt pocket and fobbed the glass entry door. The door buzzed and unlocked. He then noted that a security camera panned back and forth, slowly, aimed right at them.

Kwon, fully aware of the camera, insisted on walking across the lobby unassisted, quickly and directly to the elevator.

As they rode to the ninth floor, he leaned into the corner and Keahi again held him up with one hand, inconspicuously. There was a camera in the elevator, too.

Once in his condominium, Keahi again carried Kwon, this time from the doorway to the couch, where he deposited him, in a sitting position, gently.

Again Kwon pressed the palms of his hands against his temples. He rocked on the edge of the center cushion, moaning softly.

Keahi set the keys on the coffee table. Under other circumstances, he would have commented on Kwon's keychain, a small telescope about one-and-a-half inches long.

"You're going to have one hell of a hangover."

"I could live with a hangover, but I'm going to be sicker than that."

"Do you have a temperature? Is it the flu?"

"No. It's my medication, the methotrexate."

"What?"

"I'm not supposed to drink alcohol."

"You've got to be kidding me!"

"I wish I was," Kwon said, moaning. He now lay on his side on the couch. His stomach rumbled.

"Do you want me to take you to Kaiser, to the emergency room?"

"So they can stick me with an I.V.? No thanks. I'll survive, unless I've damaged my liver."

"You had margaritas, knowing that it could damage your liver?"

Keahi wanted to add *Why would you do something so stupid?*, but he controlled himself.

"It's *my* liver."

Keahi got Kwon a glass of ice water and found a clean sheet in the bedroom closet. As he covered Kwon with the sheet, he said "I'll stay here with you?" He was surprised that his voice cracked.

He expected Kwon to say thanks, but he didn't. Nevertheless, Keahi turned out the lights and collapsed into the chair next to Kwon and the couch.

He recalled the many nights that he had sat up next to Daniel during his last days. Tears flowed silently down his cheeks in the darkness.

And then, out of the blue, Kwon said, "I have another confession to make."

Keahi raised an eyebrow, not knowing what to expect.

"I've been investigating Masako's father, Mr. Junichiro Yasukuni."

Keahi, tired, let his eyes adjust to the darkness. He noted that Kwon had sat up to drink the ice water. "And?"

"He's a gangster."

"Really?"

"You heard me. I think her father's a gangster."

"You're kidding me, right?"

"No." In the darkness, Keahi could just make out Kwon rotating his throbbing head, side-to-side, stretching his neck, slowly. Yes, he was sitting up.

"He's in the wedding business, Kwon."

"He was also on Hawaii's Land Use Commission," Kwon said. "Appointed by the governor and approved by the state senate."

"You seem to know a lot about Mr. Yasukuni."

"I know he had the authority to redistrict land."

"Redistrict?"

"Yes, change the zoning. The Land Use Commission was a statewide zoning board. And for a while, Mr. Yasukuni was acting chairman. He determined what land would be agricultural, rural, urban, or set aside for conservation districts."

"I didn't know there was a commission like that," Keahi said.

"It was created back in the early sixties."

Kwon set the empty glass on the coffee table. He then lay down again.

"I think he helped 'business associates' convert agricultural land to urban land use."

"Why are you so interested in him? What did he do to you?" Keahi got up from his chair and pulled the sheet over Kwon. "Just because he served on the Land Use Commission doesn't make him a crook. I'm sure a lot of good people served on that commission over the years."

Kwon was quiet for a moment, perhaps organizing his thoughts.

Keahi felt suddenly blue. Why had Kwon gone out of his way to dig up something bad about Masako's father? To hurt her?

Kwon spoke again. "Remember when I was investigating the owners of the warehouse where the smugglers hid their Freon?"

"Yes."

"Remember you let me use your software to track down the owners of that warehouse?"

"Yes."

"Well, after I did that, I checked Mr. Yasukuni's assets, too."

"That's an invasion of privacy," Keahi warned. His voice expressed his disappointment and disapproval.

"You'd be surprised at his assets."

"I doubt it. He's a successful businessman."

"Too successful," Kwon said sarcastically.

"But that doesn't make him a crook. Being rich isn't a crime."

"Rich is an understatement!" Kwon said.

At that moment, Keahi recalled a rude comment Kwon had made at the bar about Masako's brother inheriting her father's estate. "You know," Keahi said, "this goes way beyond—"

"I had to do it," Kwon said, interrupting him. "I had no choice."

"And why the hell is that?" Keahi asked.

Kwon shuddered under the sheet.

"Because I love her. I'm in love with her."

Keahi's jaw dropped open and for a moment he was speechless.

Then he remembered the love potion that Kwon received in Chinatown. "You know, if you had taken that love potion tonight, on top of all the alcohol and your medications, it would probably have killed you."

"I did."

Keahi's mouth was open, gaping in disbelief.

Kwon moaned into his pillow. "I used it when I bought a round of drinks."

So that's why you drank the margaritas—to use the love potion. Keahi wanted to reach over and tuck the sheet under Kwon's chin, but he didn't. Instead, he said, "Get some sleep."

After that Keahi sat dumbfounded in the chair until Kwon began to snore. Then he quietly let himself out of the condominium and went back to his studio.

CHAPTER EIGHT

Another month passed and the team gathered at Keahi's apartment for barbecued kebobs. The occasion was the Merrie Monarch Festival, and Masako, Limen and Toi were gathered in Keahi's studio, watching the hula dancers compete on television.

After the success of the last outing, the team had decided that they would continue to take turns choosing restaurants. Keahi thought that Masako had made a good choice: the sushi had been *ono*, the bar hopping fun, and the karaoke invigorating. It was now his turn and he wanted to share his love for barbecue and dancing.

So he was now poolside preparing his new grill. The large round Weber kettle was yellow and shiny with a porcelain-enamel finish, and it was raised to his waist level on three steel legs. His old grill was in the dumpster.

Lim was drinking a Heineken, sitting poolside.

Kwon was sipping a glass of Hawaiian ice tea. He was nestled into an outdoor lounge recliner in the shade provided by a second floor lanai that projected out towards the pool. He was keeping his scarred legs in the shade, and he was still close enough to talk with Keahi and Kwon, comfortably.

"Lim, how's Limen doing?" Keahi asked.

"Fine," Lim swigged his beer, shifted in his poolside chair. "And the baby is fine, too."

"Due in August, right?"

"Yes, in five months."

Keahi adjusted the hot coals with long metal tongs. He then set the cooking grate above the fire.

"I read that four-month-old fetuses are covered with hair," Kwon ventured. "Just like little apes!"

Keahi shot Kwon a disapproving frown.

Lim, fortunately, took the rude remark as a joke. He stood up and held his arms over his head. His black swim trunks sported a wide white waistline, giving the impression that his underpants were showing. "Kwon, do you see *any* hair on this body?" He turned slowly, 360 degrees. His exposed body was tanned. "No. Now, look at yourself."

They both looked at Kwon, who also looked at himself: hairy arms, hairy legs, tufts of hair on his shoulders and upper back, and a hairy chest. Red and pink scars were visible on his legs. His fused elbow cocked outward.

Funny that he's so hairy, Keahi thought. After all, he was Korean.

Kwon smiled just enough so that one corner of his mouth came up and wrinkles crinkled around the corners of his eyes. He cupped his arthritic hands together and rested them gently on his lap.

"I guess we know who the ape is," Lim quipped. "Don't we?"

"I'm going upstairs to get the kebobs," Keahi interjected before Kwon could retort. "Don't mess with my grill."

Barefoot, he walked quickly across the warm flagstone deck to the side of his building. Then he raced up three flights of concrete stairs and down a concrete hallway to his studio.

He stepped through his doorway and paused for a moment in the short entryway, peeking into his large studio room. Toi was seated in a blue patio chair carried in from the lanai, watching a *halau*—a dance group—perform on the flat screen. Masako and Limen were seated on his big green hide-a-bed couch, at right angles to the television and the performance.

Deciding not to interrupt the performance, Keahi turned and stepped into his kitchen. He opened the door to the old white refrigerator and lifted out three pans of skewered kebobs—chicken, beef, and shrimp—and set them on the white countertop. Then he rummaged through the lower cupboards for a large platter.

He heard the jingle of a commercial as the Merry Monarch Festival broke for advertisers. Immediately, someone muted the roaring television.

Then he heard Toi say to Masako and Limen, "The world seems different now. Don't you think?"

"How do you mean?" Limen replied.

"Since the oil spill, the world doesn't seem . . . ? I don't know, it's changed, yeah?"

"Discombobulated?" Limen suggested.

"Yes, my whole life is confused," Toi said, laughing softly.

"That's such a funny word 'discombobulated,'" Masako said.

"I know what it means, now," Toi said.

"How's the baby?" Masako asked.

"Honey, the little guy is sucking his thumb!" Limen replied.

"No!"

"Yes!"

"How do you know?"

"I saw it on a sonogram. That's how I know he's a boy, too."

"Really?" Toi was awestruck.

"And his eyelashes are growing!"

"No!"

"Oh, yes! And his heart is beating twice as fast as ours. That's what the doctor says."

And Kwon says he's as hairy as an ape, Keahi thought, still listening from the kitchen.

He found a large platter for the kebobs in an overhead cabinet and his barbecue utensils in a bottom drawer. From the drawer he also took out a roll of aluminum foil.

When he turned around, Toi was standing behind him. He jumped and the utensils rattled on the platter.

"Thanks for inviting us," she said. She stepped to the sink and filled a glass with water.

"Hey, glad you could come."

"Can I help?"

"No—no thanks—I've got it under control."

"I heard from Liko," she said.

"How's he doing?" Keahi tried not to sound too interested.

"He's graduating with his class. His grades weren't the greatest, but at least he'll get his diploma." Toi seemed pleased.

Keahi thought about that for a moment.

"He's decided to travel," she added.

So he won't be returning for the summer. Liko had spent his last two summers in Hawaii. *I wonder if he is still upset about the drowning at Shark's Cove*, Keahi thought. "So he won't be enrolling in the university?"

"No," Toi said. "He wants to see Europe."

"Europe?"

"Yeah. Your great-aunt must be bankrolling him."

"He's a lucky guy!" Keahi said, but then he immediately wondered if he had said the wrong thing. After all, he didn't know how Toi felt about it. A year had passed since she had last seen Liko. And now he was leaving for Europe!

"Why Europe?" Keahi asked. "Why not Japan or China or Thailand?"

"I have no idea," Toi replied.

"Maybe you and I should go to Vegas," Keahi suggested. "See him graduate."

"No, no," Toi said, adamantly rejecting his offer. "I'll send him a card."

Keahi saw concern on her face, distinct lines of worry.

He tore off three sheets of aluminum foil and covered the three trays of beef, chicken, and shrimp kebobs. Then he stacked the trays and set them on top of the large platter and set the barbeque utensils on top of everything.

Toi opened the front door for him.

"Thanks," he said, giving her a smile. "I'll yell when the kebobs are done."

Loaded down, he walked slowly down the hall, and then stepped carefully down the outdoor stairs and back to the pool and grill.

He found Kwon still sitting in the shade, his disfigured hands still resting in his lap. He had fallen asleep.

Lim, however, was floating on his back in the middle of the pool, his face and hairless chest exposed to the bright Hawaiian sun. He was working on his already deep tan, which he probably got while on his catamaran, Keahi thought.

Keahi set the platter and trays and barbecue utensils on a plastic table next to his shiny yellow grill. After checking the coals and making sure they were just right, he skillfully transferred the first dozen marinated beef kebobs to the circular cooking grate. They sizzled and seared and flames licked up and over and around the beef, onions, and green peppers. He brushed on extra marinade that had dripped to the bottom of the pan. He smothered the flames with the shiny yellow lid. Pleased and happy, he sat down in a chair next to Kwon in the shade.

Everything is going well, he thought.

A few minutes later, his friends Carol and Angelica arrived with pork ribs and homemade barbeque sauce. Keahi had invited them, hoping they would enjoy meeting his workmates.

He awoke Kwon and introduced him first.

When Carol shook Kwon's arthritic hand, he winced and withdrew in pain.

"Your hand is so warm!" she said.

Keahi noticed that Kwon's knuckles were swollen; several were twice their normal size. Moreover, his wrists were disfigured: the result of his own body attacking itself.

Carol stared at Kwon's scarred legs.

Keahi suddenly felt apprehensive. What if his friends didn't like each other? After all, they had little in common. Angelica and Carol were both artists—Angelica a poet and Carol a professional body builder. Both lifted weights. Kwon, on the other hand, was a frustrated astronomer, with a strong, if sometimes warped, sense of justice and fairness. He had abandoned his passion for astronomy years ago, and was now hibernating as a bureaucrat in the department's clean air unit.

And their love lives were strikingly different. Angelica and Carol were inseparable—firmly committed, deeply in love. There was passion, both emotional and physical in their relationship. Kwon, on the other hand, was a loner who had fallen into a frustrating love-hate relationship with Masako. And Masako, for her part, was uninterested in a lasting romantic relationship—especially with Kwon, who she probably thought was subhuman. She needed constant stimulation. If she met a new guy at today's barbecue she would flash him a smile, but she would never flash her smile at Kwon.

Lim pulled himself out of the pool, and Keahi introduced him to Carol and Angelica. Keahi was not as concerned about Lim. He didn't care if Carol and Angelica liked or disliked him. In fact, he hadn't made up his own mind, yet. He hadn't known Lim very long, and after the incident with the labs and the performance sampling, Keahi didn't trust him.

The performance sampling had been the team's first project together. It was supposed to be a team project, but Lim had worked solo and kept the team in the dark. Worst of all, he had taken all the credit for discovering that a lab was 'cooking the books.' And then the lab had burned down just before an FBI raid; if it hadn't, Lim would have received the State Employee of the Year Award.

Lim was invited to the barbecue only because he was a member of the cleanup team, and just barely: he was on a kind of probation. He was only on the team because Jack had interceded on his behalf.

For now, Keahi let Carol and Angelica and Kwon and Lim talk story, while he focused his attention on the beef kebobs, brushing on extra chili sauce marinade, generously. Next, he brushed a teriyaki-pineapple marinade on the chicken kebobs. Then he checked the temperature of the grill. It was perfect; he was able to hold his hand over the coals for a maximum of four seconds. He closed the large yellow lid.

After that, he yelled up to his third floor lanai for Limen, Toi and Masako: "Kebobs are ready!"

Masako and Toi came down, carrying a *pahu hula*, a shark skin drum. It was a handcrafted antique, carved from a coconut log. They set it near the pool, resting the narrow base on the rough flagstone. Keahi grimaced. The shark skin was taut across the top of the drum, which was as wide as his chest. The lower portion of the drum was decorated with simple ornamentation. Masako straddled the drum and tapped on the taut shark skin, boldly.

Keahi walked over and placed a dry beach towel beneath the drum. At the same time he introduced Masako and Toi to Carol and Angelica.

Then Limen, who had been watching all the introductions and activities from the third-floor lanai—she had waved a greeting—came down with a large sack that contained two bamboo rattles, or *pu 'ili*, which she gave to

Carol and Angelica; two pairs of foot-long koa wood hula sticks, or *ka laʻau*, which she gave to Lim and Kwon; and an *ipu hula*, which she kept.

Carol and Angelica immediately started tapping the foot-and-a-half long bamboo rattles against the sides of their legs, on the top of their thighs and the palm of their hands. The split bamboo rattled and encouraged Lim and Kwon to clack the koa sticks together. The guys, at first, had trouble following the rhythm, but when Masako joined in, boldly drumming the shark skin drum, everyone soon fell into a loud, steady beat.

Keahi felt torn. On one hand he felt wonderful: the old instruments were bringing his friends together and their irregular, offbeat music delighted him. On the other hand, he was worried about the instruments. They were all pieces from his aunt's personal collection, but only Carol and Angelica knew that. Lim, Masako, and Limen had no idea that they were playing museum pieces.

And now Limen, four months pregnant, joined in with the *ipu hula*, tapping it gently. The two gourds—a large one and a smaller one, fastened together into one instrument—made a mellow sound.

"You guys be careful," he cautioned. "They're antiques, the genuine articles."

"What's the matter?" Limen asked. "You afraid I'll thump your *ipu* against this stone deck?"

"Oh Lord," Keahi said, "pleeease don't do that."

"I'll be careful," Limen said, holding the *ipu* by an attached cord, cradling it on top of her bare feet. She smiled at Keahi and added, "It's so heavy, though. Maybe I drop it?"

"No, you will not," Keahi said, aware that she was only teasing him. "If you drop it I will throw you in the pool. Even if you *are* pregnant."

"One moment," Keahi said, suddenly thinking of something. "I'll be right back."

He sprinted upstairs to his studio and returned with his nose flute, and together they made music, with Toi joining in on the ukulele.

Keahi was ecstatic! He loved the antique instruments. And the sound of the instruments, played by his friends, filled him with joy.

Soon the neighbors ventured out onto their lanais, attracted by both the sound of the Hawaiian instruments and the smell of barbecue.

After a while, Keahi set the nose flute aside, turned and basted the kebobs, and then started dancing the ancient hulas. His neighbors watched from their lanais or they gathered poolside, pulled up chairs, sat on the edge of planters or on the flagstone pool deck, dangled their feet into the cool pool water and enjoyed the free entertainment.

Keahi started with a chant he had learned as a boy, but then he surprised everyone and performed a new chant about nature's ability to rebound from man's folly. He had written the chant for Toi, to give her hope that Hanauma Bay would recover. Everyone applauded.

Afterwards, while they were eating the kebobs and ribs—everyone who came to listen was invited to eat, too—Keahi watched the interaction between Carol and Angelica and his coworkers.

He noticed that Masako took an immediate dislike to Carol and Angelica. Their deep attachment to each other seemed to disturb her. He sensed that she felt threatened—no, challenged—challenged to show that she was cleverer, more personable, more beautiful. She became frustrated at their general indifference to her and managed only to behave badly, even rudely. Keahi sat and watched as her frustration turned to bad behavior, and she became sulky. Usually it was Kwon who brought out the worst in her. Today it was Masako's own vanity. *I guess she won't teach them to pole dance*, he thought, smiling.

Keahi also observed Lim, who appeared uncomfortable when Angelica and Carol kissed or touched. He averted his eyes when they dried each other off with their brightly colored beach towels. *What is he thinking?* Keahi wondered. His behavior confirmed what Keahi had suspected for a long time: that Lim was uneasy with Keahi's homosexuality, too.

Kwon, on the other hand, always in the pursuit of truth—even when the pursuit wasn't politically correct—said more than one thing that upset Carol and Angelica, and he asked too many questions, but they seemed to take it in stride, more or less. Eventually, however, they threw him into the pool. His arthritis and scarred legs didn't stop them. And everyone applauded. Amazingly, Kwon enjoyed it, laughing louder than everyone else. *Perhaps they will become friends*, Keahi thought, hopefully.

Kwon and Masako, though, kept their distance from each other. Kwon stayed in the shade as much as possible, hiding his body from the sun, and Masako in the sun, slathered in sunscreen, wearing a pair of aviator tints—expensive Bulgari sunglasses. Her skin was milky white.

Soon the chicken kebobs and beef kebobs and shrimp kebobs were eaten. Toi's potato salad, Masako's artichoke and rice dish, Limen's local style coleslaw, and Carol and Angelica's pork ribs disappeared, too.

And then Keahi was once again alone.

CHAPTER NINE

KEAHI FOUND THE TEAM WATCHING the Kamehameha Day parade at the corner of Kalakaua Avenue and Lili'uokalani Avenue in Waikiki. He noted that the usual gaggle of tourists was conspicuously absent, and only a few locals had turned out.

"Sorry I kept you guys waiting," he said as he approached.

Toi looked up at him from her seat on the curb. "Where have you been?" she chided, smiling.

He extended his hand and helped her up, then gave her a comforting hug and a warm kiss on the left cheek.

"The parade is almost over."

Her friendly admonishment stung, especially since he was tired and hungover. Last night he had stayed up, seated in a lounge chair on his lanai, drinking beer until he passed out. He had wallowed in a melancholy funk, imagining what his life could have been if only he had followed his dreams. And late morning, when he had awakened, his regrets had morphed into a pounding headache. He had almost stayed home to recover, and it was his indecision that had made him late: should he stay in the dark studio, or join his friends under the bright Hawaiian sun? Fortunately, his dark-tinted polarized sunglasses helped.

"You didn't miss anything," Kwon said, yawning, bored by the anemic parade. "This parade is dead. Worse than the lion dances."

"Then let's eat," Toi suggested.

"Hey," Kwon said, "it's my turn to choose a restaurant, right?"

Keahi's stomach surged as he anticipated kimchi.

"Everyone is tired of eating Korean barbecue, right? Too much plate lunch that." Kwon thought a moment, then continued, "Let's do Trailok's Thai, okay?"

"Great idea!" Keahi quickly seconded the suggestion. "A pot of tea would be nice."

Everyone concurred.

So, as high noon approached, Keahi adjusted his sunglasses and the team trudged across Waikiki to Trailok's Thai. They had no reservations, but when they arrived, the popular restaurant was all but empty. They paused at the entrance, debating whether they should go elsewhere. They almost left.

After they were seated and ordered, Keahi asked, "Limen, how is the baby?"

"I've had problems breathing." Limen explained how the weight of the baby was putting pressure on the bottom of her rib cage. "Sometimes I can't catch my breath. Earlier this morning, as we were watching the parade, he was kicking and punching. If he keeps working his legs and arms, maybe he will be a weightlifter like you, Keahi."

Keahi smiled. Her comment pleased him.

"His eyes are open," Limen added. "That's what the doctor said."

"But it's too dark in there to see anything," Keahi remarked, his face filled with amazement.

The team and Limen laughed.

But then Limen jumped in her chair. "He kicked! He heard your joke, Uncle Keahi."

Again everyone laughed and Keahi chuckled.

"Toi, how are *you* doing?" Keahi asked, directing the attention away from himself.

"I'm seeing a counselor, which I should have done months ago. And I'm taking medications." She explained that the medications were temporary, just until she recovered her equilibrium.

"And I can sleep again!" she added.

"Oh!" Masako lamented. "What I would give for a good night's sleep!"

"Me too," Keahi agreed, still stiff from waking up in a lounge chair.

Their food arrived and they began eating.

Keahi picked at his green papaya salad. "Toi, heard anything from Liko?"

"You mean Mr. Gadabout Europe? A couple of postcards—one from Spain, another from Argentina. He said he was going to Chile next."

"Chile? What in the world's in Chile?"

"He didn't say. He just said it was his next stop."

"So now he's in South America..." Keahi murmured. He poured himself a cup of tea.

"Is that Hawaiian music I hear?" Lim asked, trying to add something to the conversation. The music was coming in low over strategically placed speakers.

"A local group," Keahi answered.

"You should never have given up your music," Lim added.

"I don't know." Keahi smiled. "How does one make a living chanting while wearing a big white diaper?"

"Start your own *halau*," Masako suggested.

"Yes, lots of people would sign up for your classes," Toi added. "You've got five people right here."

Keahi looked at his teammates and tried to imagine them dancing hula. He chuckled. "Thank you, but that opportunity has passed." *And there's no time to start from zero.*

Keahi noticed that Kwon was unusually quiet. "Kwon, what about *your* dream?"

"My dream?"

"Astronomy?" Keahi knew that Kwon had a star map in his cubicle, and beautiful photographs of novae and galaxies on the walls of his apartment. Keahi also recalled how Kwon used to talk about celestial things—the planets and sun and stars.

Kwon's face instantly changed, became more pensive. Keahi immediately regretted his question.

"I dropped out of school. I had to help my family." Kwon paused a moment, then added: "I never finished my dissertation."

"Why not go back to school?" Toi suggested.

"I still support my father."

"I didn't know you had family here," Toi said.

"I don't. My father is in Los Angeles. My mother, she died before the riots—the riots in Los Angeles. For that I'm thankful. She didn't live to see my father lose everything... his gas station, their home."

"What happened?" Lim asked.

Keahi could see the curiosity in Lim's face. But it wasn't an interest in Kwon's family. *He wants to know why the business failed.*

"Well," Kwon said, glancing at Masako, "the story starts with my grandfather, when he was living in Korea at the beginning of the last century." Kwon ran his finger through the condensation on the outside of his water glass and sighed. Then he looked at Lim. "Are you really interested?"

"Yes," Lim said. "I am."

"Me too." Toi nodded agreement.

When Kwon looked his way, Keahi nodded for him to tell the story, too.

Kwon's gaze then returned to Masako.

She was not paying attention.

Keahi could tell that pissed off Kwon—and motivated him, obviously, because in the almost empty restaurant, with the sound of Hawaiian music playing from ceiling-mounted speakers, Kwon began his story, starting with his grandfather. "He was very happy in Korea. And he would have stayed there, too." Kwon looked directly and pointedly at Masako. When she made eye contact, he said, "But the Japanese invaded."

Masako shifted her focus to Keahi and spoke to him with her eyes, "Here he goes again! More about the Evil-Empire!"

And then Kwon explained. At the beginning of the century, the Japanese invaded Korea, abolished the Korean monarchy, seized private businesses, and stole private property—in short, Japan conquered, occupied and then dismantled Korea.

"They stole everything my grandfather had. He resisted. They killed his parents and brothers and sisters. The Japanese killed his entire family. So he fled to China. Then to Hawaii. In Hawaii, he hoped to carry on Korea's struggle for independence. Instead, he found himself working on a sugar plantation. It was backbreaking work and low wages—you guys have heard what the plantations were like—but worst of all, he found himself working side-by-side *with* the Japanese, and I mean Japanese labor gangs. Can you imagine that? Japanese immigrants were working in the same sugar fields as my father! He couldn't accept that."

The team listened as Kwon told the story about how his grandfather left the plantation and sought work in downtown Honolulu. But, because of discrimination and a lack of education and training, he was unable to find a job. So he bought a one-way boat ticket to California, where he picked fruits and vegetables up and down the coast with other *umin.*

"The first time my grandfather saw my grandmother, she was in a peach tree, picking peaches. She was twenty years younger."

Keahi imagined a young girl, standing on a ladder, picking fuzzy peaches. He also imagined a middle-aged man in his late thirties, standing beside her wooden ladder and gazing up at her, falling in love with her. He saw the man smiling, shyly, and the girl holding a soft, ripe peach in her hand.

Kwon told how they had combined their meager incomes, saved some money, joined the Korean community in Los Angeles, and opened a small shoe repair store.

"And then my father was born. Yes, he was born an American! He was in Los Angeles, working in a gas station, when

Japan attacked Pearl Harbor." Kwon looked at Masako again. "My father enlisted in the army and fought against Japan. This made my grandfather very happy."

Kwon paused and looked around him. The team was sitting quietly, listening to his story. Masako was annoyed. Something just shy of anger clouded her face.

"Lim, the GI Bill gave my father his first real break. He went to the University of California on the GI Bill and earned a bachelor's degree in business. Then, after his graduation, an oil company hired him to manage a gas station in Oklahoma. Later, the oil company sent him back to school, at the University of Kansas, in Lawrence, where he earned his Master's in Business Administration. After that, he managed a chain of gas stations for the oil company. Then he decided to strike out on his own."

"So, he moved back to my grandparents' neighborhood in Los Angeles and opened his own independent gas station in an area known as Korea Town. My grandfather was very proud of him. He was an American success story: a university graduate, a successful manager, and the owner and operator of his own full-service gas station."

"My father invested heavily in Korea Town. As a result, he was well-known and respected. And he shared his success; my grandfather encouraged him to help recent Korean immigrants start small businesses, and my father did."

"So what went wrong?" Lim asked.

"In his eagerness to help, he overextended himself."

"And then the riots?" Keahi suggested.

"Exactly," Kwon agreed, sadly. "At that time, I was attending the University, working on my PhD in astronomy."

"And you left school to help your father?" Keahi asked.

"Yes. He had a stroke during the riots. He was working at his gas station when things got crazy...."

Keahi looked at Kwon's eyes and saw anger.

And disappointment.

And pain.

Kwon explained that his father's hospital costs and his other medical bills, including the cost of his father's extended stay in a skilled nursing home, had consumed the family's savings, making it impossible for Kwon to continue his PhD. In addition, his father's investments had been made to small businessmen in Korea Town—businessmen who would never be able to repay personal loans because they too had lost everything. The rioters destroyed their businesses and their lives, too.

And now Keahi felt a sadness coming off Kwon like spray off ocean waves.

And then he thought about his own life choices and decisions. *I have no excuse for not following my dreams, for wasting my talents, for squandering my opportunities.*

His headache wasn't quite as bad now; the pot of hot tea had helped.

"I have some news," Keahi said.

"What?" Kwon asked.

"Pete's quit."

"Again," Lim quipped.

The dig hurt and Keahi tried not to flinch. "A private maritime company hired him. They want him to beef up their emergency response group."

"No kidding," Lim said. His voice now reflected admiration.

"Yeah, he told me last night." *I should have seen it coming,* Keahi thought. "He sounded very excited."

"I'm going to miss his enthusiasm," Masako said.

"Well," Kwon said. "I'm going to miss him too. He's the only other person, besides me, who speaks his mind and says what he means."

Shut up, Keahi thought.

Pete had stopped by after work on Thursday and told Keahi that he wasn't going to work on Friday. And he didn't. He obviously still felt no obligation to give Santos notice that he was quitting. That's the way he had quit the first time after the meth lab explosion. Keahi still fondly recalled how Pete had told Santos off that time. After Santos complained that he deserved more respect than such a short notice, Pete had answered back something like, "I give respect to those who deserve it." And now he had quit without even coming into the office. Santos was furious!

"He didn't even have to clean out his office this time," Keahi said, chuckling.

But Pete's sudden departure wasn't the only reason that Keahi had gotten drunk last night. "My friend," Pete had said, "you are responsible for your own happiness. What's stopping you?"

CHAPTER TEN

"THIS IS WHERE I MET LIKO," Toi said to Keahi. They were seated together on a bench, looking out towards San Souci Beach and the Pacific Ocean. A single palm tree swayed behind them in the breeze. It was too skinny to provide shade.

They had kicked off their slippers, and the heels of their bare feet rested on the concrete wall separating them from the off-white sandy beach. Toi curled her toes against the rough concrete.

"Do you miss him?"

"Yes!" Toi looked at Keahi.

He smiled at her, took her hand and squeezed it. *And I miss Daniel.*

"I wish I had news." Toi sighed. "But the postcards stopped."

Keahi half-smiled, disappointed. He had hoped to catch up on Liko's adventures.

He glanced behind them, back to where Lim was sitting in a folding sling chair under a blue tarp next to a big cooler filled with ice, sodas, hotdogs and hamburgers. He appeared relaxed, watching the coals slowly turn white-hot in the bright yellow Smokey Joe that Keahi had set up for their cookout.

"It doesn't get much better than this, does it?" Keahi said. "Hotdogs and hamburgers on the grill, a walk down the beach to Fort DeRussy, and then fireworks."

The beaches in Waikiki had just reopened after being closed for seven disastrous months for a state economy so dependent on tourism. Businesses had closed, some forever. And the ecological disaster wasn't over. Reefs were dead or dying. The monk seal was, most marine experts agreed, history. The few surviving seals were in captivity, caged like the *'alala*—the Hawaiian crow. Extinct in the wild. And the beaches were now thermally treated sand. Sterilized.

"What a wonderful breeze," Toi said. Keahi glanced overhead and saw palm fronds rustling.

In front of them, two tourists—a man and a woman—sat together on the steps of a lifeguard stand. There should have been a hundred tourists sunbathing.

Then Keahi spotted Masako swimming freestyle between the beach and a windsock blowing on a pole far from shore. The pole marked a channel cut through the coral reef—a channel that once directed water to a World War I natatorium memorial. She had almost reached the pole.

"There is something magical about San Souci," Toi said.

"Yes," Keahi agreed. "It *is* still a magical place." *Even if the coral and sea life are decimated.*

There was a long, comfortable silence between them. Then Keahi said, "I'd better check on Kwon. Do you want to come?"

"No. I just want to watch the ocean."

"Want a soda or something?"

"No, I'm fine."

Keahi found Kwon where he had left him, nearby, seated at the bar in the beachside hotel. The length of the bar was perpendicular to the beach, which afforded a sideways view of the ocean.

Keahi sat down next to him on a barstool. From his seat, turning to his left, Keahi could see the windsock blowing in the distance, and then he saw Masako, and then he realized why Kwon was sitting at the bar—he was watching her swim. He was sipping gin and tonic and watching Masako swim out to the windsock and then back again.

"You drinking on top of your medicine again?"

Kwon shot Keahi an annoyed expression without really looking at him, keeping his focus outside, instead.

"You *are* still taking your medicine, aren't you?"

"It's a shot, not a pill. I don't take it. A nurse sticks a needle in my ass."

Great, Keahi thought, *you're already two sheets to the wind.* "How is your arthritis?"

"It's flaring up. And yes, I'm still taking all my medications, but they're not working as well. I've added a new one to the stew."

"Does it have side effects, too?"

"All my medicines have side effects." Kwon took a deep breath and sighed.

Keahi suspected that the 'new medication' was alcohol. "What's the matter, my friend?"

Kwon shrugged the question away. Turning his attention from the ocean and Masako to the bar, he ordered another gin and tonic, and tried to buy a Mai Tai for Keahi.

Keahi refused the Mai Tai. He let Kwon buy him a ginger ale instead.

"What we need is a hurricane," Kwon said. "A big fuckin' hurricane."

"You don't mean that."

"Yes, I do," Kwon murmured. "We need another disaster—to keep everyone together."

Keahi shook his head. "I've been thinking about all the stupid things that I've said to Masako."

"You'll be here for hours," Keahi said, jokingly, trying to lighten the conversation. He could feel the loneliness exhaling from Kwon.

"I've even thought of apologizing." He sat up straight on the bar stool. "Should I?"

Keahi raised an eyebrow. *I don't know*, he thought. *You may only make a fool of yourself and reap her scorn and derision.* He said: "She may not forgive you."

That possibility upset Kwon. He poked an ice cube in his gin and tonic and watched it sink, then rise. "But I would not expect her forgiveness."

If Masako knew that you were in love with her she would treat you like a poi dog for the cooking pot.

"Sometimes I feel so embarrassed about the things I've said, the way I've acted. I know I offended her, upset her. I feel terrible about it. But what can I do?"

Keahi saw the anguish in his friend's face, heard it in his inebriated voice.

"Sometimes I want to take it all back—all the things I've said. But she needs to know the truth."

"Know what truth?"

"The truth about Japan and her father and herself."

"Ah, yes. We've talked about that before. I didn't understand it then, and I don't understand it now."

Kwon frowned with bitter disappointment. "If *you* don't understand, Keahi, how can she?"

"I have no idea," Keahi said. He sighed. The ginger ale arrived and he now wished that he had accepted the Mai Tai.

They gazed out to the ocean and spotted Masako returning from the windsock, executing a powerful butterfly stroke.

"How does she stay in the channel?" Kwon asked. "How does she avoid the reef?"

"She's following old cables laid in the channel. Some are now buried, but some are still on top of the sand where you can see them."

"Sometimes I feel so angry—" Kwon said. "I want to grab her and shake some sense into her."

"I can't let you do that."

"I can't see you stopping me."

"Why not?"

"Because you're the most passive person I know. You couldn't shoo a pigeon."

"Maybe so, but I could still hoist your skinny ass by the back of your jeans." Keahi smiled at Kwon.

They sat quietly together for a few moments.

"Love may be a biochemical fantasy," Kwon said, swirling the ice in his gin and tonic, "but its effects are real."

"Yes, the effects *are* real," Keahi agreed. *And it can ruin your life.*

"Will this pain ever stop?"

"Let's hope so." *But mine never has!*

Together they watched Masako. She had a powerful butterfly stroke.

The afternoon passed slowly. The team grilled hotdogs and hamburgers. Kwon refused to join them. He was now pouting. He said he wasn't hungry. While the team swam and laughed and enjoyed each other's company, Kwon sat alone at the bar in the hotel, occasionally seeing one of them swim to the wind sock, occasionally getting a glimpse of Masako.

Finally, the afternoon ended and the team watched the sun turn into a large orange ball and drop into the ocean. Kwon, still seated at the bar, watched the sunset by himself.

When it was time to walk down the beach to see the fireworks, Keahi went back to the hotel bar to coax Kwon into joining them. Kwon finally capitulated. However, he was so unsteady on his feet that he needed to lean against Keahi for support. Keahi, for his part, wrapped his arm around his friend's shoulders, not only to steady him but also to give the appearance of two friends strolling down the beach together. Nevertheless, Kwon's legs were such wet noodles that it was obvious he was drunk.

"I have decided to apologize to her," Kwon said, slurring his words.

"I don't know, my friend. Maybe you should wait—another time. Perhaps when you are alone with her. Not while everyone is here."

"I embarrassed her in public; I will apologize to her in public."

When they rejoined the team in front of the natatorium—that is, where the natatorium use to be—Kwon pulled away from Keahi and tried to stand by himself. At first, his friends thought he wobbled because of the arthritis in his knees. Then they realized he was drunk.

Keahi saw Toi and Lim's expression change. They were visibly upset.

"I have something to tell Masako," Kwon announced, pronouncing each word slowly, carefully. "Where is she?"

"She has gone ahead," Toi said.

"Jus' my luck."

Together they walked under the heavy branches of the hau trees, branches originally trained to grow on a rusty metal arbor that use to run the length of the demolished natatorium. After that, they cut across a grassy field to the sea wall, where they followed the beach walk behind the Waikiki Aquarium, passing the spot where Keahi had first seen Toi and Liko seated together on the rough concrete wall, watching the sunset, listening to the Makiki Sons benefit concert.

Keahi recalled how good they had looked together: Liko's tan and muscular body seated next to Toi's svelte softness. Yes, it would have made a picturesque postcard.

Next they passed Queen's Beach, where Keahi looked for familiar faces but recognized none. He felt disappointed. But then he realized that he was looking for Daniel's handsome face and masculine body—a sensuous body that rivaled Donatello's David. A body that now existed only in bronze. And memory.

The team took off their slippers and walked in the sand. Occasionally the waves washed over their feet and splashed up their calves, sometimes to their knees. There was occasionally black oil in the sand—probably washed in from offshore—and the soles of their feet turned black.

Toi spotted the first star. "I see a star!"

"Where?"

"Over there." She pointed out over the ocean, high above the horizon.

Kwon said it was Venus, not a star, so no wishes were made. It was a slipper moon and Venus.

They passed stacks of colorful surfboards racked vertically at Kuhio Beach, went around a snack bar closed due to lack of business, and walked across the beach behind the Ala Moana Surfrider Hotel.

They almost lost Kwon when they passed Duke's. The music was loud and Kwon wanted to go inside for another drink, but Keahi talked him out of it—told him that he would miss the fireworks, which reminded Kwon that he wanted to apologize to Masako. So they continued.

Soon they passed the new, manicured beach behind the Royal Hawaiian Hotel, where pink umbrellas and pink lounge chairs rested behind a rope dividing the Royal Hawaiian's property and the public beach area. The hotel guests had already left the beach for the day—some to dinner, some to the fireworks, some to find other entertainment.

The team continued until they arrived at Fort DeRussy Beach. The beach was already crowded with locals, sitting on the kind of grass mats that sold for about a dollar. Keahi took a deep breath.

As they looked around for Masako, he tried to imagine Kwon apologizing to her in front of this large crowd. Being so drunk, Kwon would enjoy that. Keahi sighed. Then he spotted her.

She was with Samy, the independently wealthy guy who never worked. Although he was casually dressed, his clothes looked new; his shirt still sported the original creases. His khaki shorts looked first-time-worn, too. Even his tennis shoes were white and unsoiled and spotless. He appeared proud, self-confident, and very pleased with himself.

Poor Kwon, Keahi thought.

"I see her," Kwon announced publicly.

The fireworks were huge. Not that they were better than previous years, no. But this year the colorful explosions were an outlet for everyone's pent-up emotions. Keahi cried, silently, wiping away tears.

After the grand finale Masako's boyfriend suggested they walk down the beach, back to Duke's. Kwon, ironically, also wanted to go.

"I would," Masako said, "but I'm too tired."

Samy flashed a disappointed expression.

"I overdid my swim," she explained. "I'm exhausted."

The team agreed: everyone was tired, so they said goodnight.

As they turned to leave, Samy grabbed Masako's forearm.

"What?" she said, sharply, startled.

"Let's you and me go to Duke's."

"I'm too tired." She pulled loose and turned to leave.

And again Samy grabbed her arm. But this time he jerked her around. "Don't turn your back on me."

She pried his fingers from her arm. "What's the matter with you!"

He reached for her again, but she backed up, just out of his reach.

He stepped forward.

But Kwon wedged between them, the palms of his hands against Samy's chest and his back to Masako.

Kwon pushed.

Samy flew backwards and fell onto the sand. But then he sprang to his feet and stepped up to Kwon. His fist shook inches from Kwon's face.

Kwon stood his ground.

Samy stepped back, mumbled something, turned to leave.

Kwon exhaled a sigh of relief. He smiled, pleased with himself. He turned to face Masako.

And then Samy false cracked him to the side of his head. Kwon dropped to the sand like a coconut. Knocked out.

Masako screamed.

Samy stood there a moment, shaking his wrist in pain. Perhaps it was broken. But then he turned and ran, his feet kicking up sand as he fled down the beach towards Diamond Head.

Keahi, hearing Masako yell, "What's the matter with you?" had spun around in time to see Kwon do his wedgy and push-hands. Amazing. He wondered if the move had been an accident or whether Kwon knew tai chi. He guessed the former: just luck.

And then Keahi had seen the sucker punch, had seen Kwon's feet crumple beneath him. He had rushed over, but Samy was already running.

"What a jerk!" Masako exclaimed. She knelt over Kwon.

Keahi's eyes traced a string of blood drops in the sand back to Kwon's nose, which was split and folded sideways on his face, broken.

A military guy from the crowd stepped forward and said, "He may have a concussion. He needs a doctor, an emergency room. My car is nearby—"

Kwon opened his eyes. "What happened?"

"You okay?" Masako asked, kneeling beside him.

Startled to find her so close, looking into his eyes, he blushed.

"You idiot!" she snapped.

He thinks that he has redeemed himself, Keahi thought. *Poor guy.*

"Thanks for the offer," Masako said to the military guy, who was hovering above her, "but we can take him to the hospital." She looked at Keahi for confirmation.

"My car is back at San Souci," Keahi answered. He had used it to transport the grill. It was parked at the other end of Waikiki.

Masako looked at Toi. "I parked along Kalakaua Avenue, near the aquarium," Toi said. That was also at the other end of Waikiki.

She turned to Lim. "I rode the bus so I wouldn't have to fight the traffic," Lim quickly explained. "I never ride the bus, but made an exception today."

"And I parked at the Hale Koa garage." She turned so that only Keahi could see her face, and then mouthed the word 'damn!'

Keahi shrugged with his palms up and hands pointing towards her. His body said 'Sorry kid, but you're the closest.'

She turned to the military guy and feigned a look of helplessness.

"The traffic will be terrible," the military guy predicted. "I can call an ambulance."

"I don't want an ambulance," Kwon said, holding his nose. He had been quiet until now.

Keahi could tell that Masako was biting her tongue.

"Time is burning," Kwon quipped.

"You idiot!" she snapped, losing it. "That was a stupid thing to do."

Kwon beamed with happiness.

Keahi thought, *Kwon, shut up! If you're smart, you won't push your luck. Right now Masako feels obligated. But it's a tenuous obligation. A very tenuous obligation.*

They helped Kwon to his feet. Blood ran from his nose to his chin and dripped. Keahi thought that the drops of blood in the sand looked like red cinnamon hearts.

"Tilt your head back," Masako ordered.

Kwon obeyed. He took off his T-shirt and leaned backwards, covering his nose with it. Tears welled up in his eyes.

"Blood is running down my throat," he complained.

Keahi's eyes traced the flow. Blood had run down Kwon's chin and neck and into the hair on his upper chest. *One bloody hairy monkey*, Keahi thought, recalling Lim's comments from several weeks ago.

"I'll go with you guys," Toi volunteered.

"Thanks," Masako said, "but there's not enough room in my car."

She must have driven her convertible, Keahi thought.

Kwon's T-shirt quickly saturated with blood, and blood dripped onto the metal steps as they took a shortcut up the Hale Koa's escalator to the hotel's lobby, then out through the main entrance.

Hotel guests stared.

They reached the garage, and, as Masako had said, there was room in her BMW for only two persons. The team helped Kwon into the passenger seat, and Masako got in and powered down the windows.

"I'll take him to Kaiser's emergency room."

Keahi glanced at Kwon. He was holding his nose with his blood-soaked T-shirt, sitting upright, tilting his head backward against the headrest. Drops of blood had dripped onto the gray, cloth floor mats of the BMW.

Keahi took off his Gold's Gym T-shirt and handed it through the window to Kwon. "To protect the inside of her car."

Kwon dropped his blood-soaked T-shirt out the passenger window onto the concrete parking deck. It literally squished when it hit the concrete. Keahi saw that Kwon's nose was deformed. Kwon tilted back his head again and covered his nose with Keahi's white T-shirt.

Masako pulled out of the parking space. She waved out her window to the team as she pulled around a corner post in the garage and disappeared from sight, driving away with Kwon.

Toi, Keahi and Lim were left standing on the fourth floor of the Hale Koa garage. They looked at each other and shook their heads in disbelief.

"We must be in the twilight zone," Keahi said.

"No kidding," Toi and Lim said simultaneously.

They walked to the bus stop at the front of the garage, where Lim said, "This is my stop. I'll see you guys tomorrow."

Then Keahi walked Toi back to her car, which was parked along the beach side of Kapiolani Park, across from the aquarium. When they reached her car, he gave her a hug and kissed her on the cheek.

After she drove away, Keahi picked up his grill where he had left it in front of San Souci beach. The coals were dead. He dumped them into the circular concrete coal bin that looked like a recycled section of storm water drainage pipe. Then he loaded the grill in his old car.

Minutes later, alone on his lanai, he grabbed a Foster's Lager out of the refrigerator. He sipped it slowly while seated in a lounge chair on his small lanai, watching the stars and the moon, focusing on the planet that looked like a bright star—Venus.

He wondered how things were going at the emergency room.

The next day, early in the morning, Keahi stopped by Kwon's place. Kwon buzzed him in through the security doors. He was wearing a big bandage on his nose, held in place with tape and gauze wrapped several times around his head. Both his eyes were black and blue.

"I apologized to Masako." He seemed pleased, as if a heavy burden had been lifted from his shoulders.

"Did she accept your apology?"

"No."

Keahi shook his head.

"You just missed her. She left about twenty minutes ago."

"She spent the night here?"

"Yes, she did."

Keahi's raised an eyebrow. "And?"

"No, she slept on the couch. The doctor said someone needed to watch me during the first twenty-four hours, so she got the job." He held up both hands. "I wish I could say that she was happy about it, but . . ."

"Are you okay?"

"Yes, except I told her that I loved her."

Keahi's other eyebrow rose. "You didn't?"

"Yes." He sighed heavily. "I did."

"And what happened?"

"She didn't say anything. She just stared at me."

"And I really screwed up this morning," he added.

"Oh God, what happened?"

"I said a few things about her father."

Again Keahi shook his head. "Like what?"

"I was encouraged. So, I told her about her father, him being a gangster and all."

Keahi shook his head, sadly.

"She didn't believe any of it."

"And now she is really pissed?"

"Yeah. She is *really* pissed. She's calling me a racist again." He paused, and then added, as a joke, "It was a good thing that my nose was already broken."

When Keahi didn't laugh or even smile, Kwon added, "And she drives like a maniac!"

That made Keahi smile, but sorrowfully.

PART THREE
DISSONANCE

CHAPTER ELEVEN

IN MID-JULY, MASAKO CALLED KEAHI and asked if she could stop by his studio. She was sobbing on her cell phone, en route from her father's house. She said her brother Vance had committed *jisatsu*. He had failed the entrance exams to Todai, the University of Tokyo. Ashamed, he had committed suicide.

She arrived a minute later.

When Keahi answered the door, he saw her eyes were red and swollen. Her arms were crossed tight against her body and her shoulders hunched as if she were cold. She was holding a white envelope.

She began talking the moment she sat down on Keahi's large green sofa. But she described her mother's death, not her brother's. Patiently, Keahi listened.

She said, "The morning after she died, no one came to wake me up, even though it was a school day. I overslept and no one noticed. I lay in bed half the morning waiting for my father to come and tell me, 'Daughter, you've overslept.

Hurry—get up or you'll be late for school.' I lay in bed waiting for him to come and wake me up. Isn't that silly? But he never came. Finally I got up, went downstairs, and made my own lunch. I felt so alone."

"After my mother died, my dad sent us to Japan. I was in the second grade. Vance was only five weeks old. He developed bronchitis during the move, and my aunt gave him *saki* to fight the congestion."

"I don't blame my father. He was a businessman. He knew nothing about raising children."

"We arrived in Kyoto during the winter. I remember it was winter, even though I was only seven-and-a-half years old. I didn't have a heavy coat or warm clothes, not even one long dress to wear. Straight from Hawaii into a harsh Japanese winter."

"My cousins made fun of me, constantly. My dad said they lived in a nice home, but I saw right away that it wasn't nice. It was a small, boxy apartment on the fifth floor. I hated climbing all those steps." Tears welled up in her eyes. "And the view outside their apartment was power lines and telephone poles. It was ugly."

"I thought that my uncle and aunt were poor. We sat on the floor when we ate dinner—on cushions around a low table. There was only one big room and *shoji* that slid on rails. At night, my aunt pulled the *shoji* to make one medium and two small rooms. Then she got mattresses out of a small closet and we slept on the floor. I thought that they were dreadfully poor. And I was brash enough to tell my aunt, and she scolded me."

"My first breakfast with them was terrible. The bread was not Loves bread and the milk tasted funny. And when I complained that the milk was bad—it did taste different—my cousins teased me. They pasteurize their milk at a higher temperature, which makes it taste funny. But when I was a kid, I didn't know that."

"When I cried, my aunt scolded me. When I said things were different in my father's house, she said that *I* was 'funny.' When I needed comfort, she ignored me."

"And my cousin—well, my cousin told the neighbors that I had killed my mother and that I had fits and that I was crazy. So I became the neighborhood weirdo."

"My brother, however, was much luckier. He was so tiny, only five weeks old. He never knew our mother so he never felt her loss. I, on the other hand, would spend hours thinking about her. I imagined that she was still alive, that she would come for us, that she would take us home. But my brother had no memories of her, so he never had that fantasy. It was easier for him."

Masako took a picture out of the white envelope and handed it to Keahi. "That's Vance. He wore that *hachimaki* all the time."

Keahi looked at the picture. Masako's brother was reading a manga.

Masako gave a weak laugh. "He thought this picture was very funny. See, on the back." Masako took the card back and turned it over and showed Keahi the note scribbled in her brother's meticulous handwriting: 'Studying hard. Your brother, Number One *Ronnin.*'

Then Masako said she and her father were leaving for Japan to attend the funeral.

"Oh Keahi, I don't want to go to the funeral. I especially don't want to stay with my aunt and uncle and cousins again. I don't want to see them."

Keahi nodded his head in understanding.

"What should I do?" Masako asked.

"Go to the funeral."

CHAPTER TWELVE

THE NEXT TIME KWON AND MASAKO saw each other was two weeks after Masako returned from Japan and her brother's funeral. It was the first week of August and the occasion was Limen giving birth to a seven pound, healthy boy. The team met at St. Francis Hospital to congratulate Lim and Limen and to see the baby.

Kwon looked like hell. He was bent over, and he was holding one elbow out to his side, stiffly. Keahi assumed that it was the arthritis.

"You look like you're in pain," Keahi said carefully.

Kwon nodded his head, grateful that someone had acknowledged his suffering.

He also looked sad. Whether the sadness was a result of his rheumatoid arthritis, his unrequited love for Masako, the effect of the long hours he and everyone else had been working, or a combination of all of the above, Keahi didn't know.

"He's one hairless buggah," Keahi said, looking at the baby. Except for his long, black eyelashes and eyebrows, the baby was bald. "He's not as hairy as you thought he would be, is he, Kwon?"

Kwon blushed red. That made the new scar on the side of his nose stand out, pale white and jagged like a bolt of lightning.

A nurse in the room cleared her throat, a clear warning to Keahi to behave himself.

Limen made baby talk, unintelligible, silly noises. She repeated a series of gah-gahs and goo-goos in a variety of different tones until she got the baby to stare at her in astonishment. "Who's a pretty little boy, eh?" She tickled the baby's stomach. His eyes were closed tight and his face was red and mashed up.

Then she asked Keahi if he wanted to hold him. He did, but he was unsure of himself. "I've never held a baby before."

From the bed, she handed him the baby anyway. Keahi cradled the baby in one arm and with his free hand rubbed the bald crown, feeling the soft spot. *So vulnerable and innocent,* he thought. *Are we all born this way?*

Because the hospital room was so small, Masako and Kwon ended up standing side-by-side. Seeing them together, Keahi tried to imagine them as a couple with their own child. It seemed highly improbable. *No,* Keahi thought to himself, *Masako's game is to avoid pain, avoid loss, avoid intimacy.*

Keahi cupped one of the baby's tiny feet in his huge hand. *He's flat-footed,* Keahi thought. *Should I say something?* He studied the baby. *His neck is too short and his head is too big.*

"You," the nurse said, "give the lady back her baby. You've held him long enough for one day."

Keahi didn't argue. In fact, he was grateful that she had interrupted his thoughts. What if he had said something inappropriate? He handed the baby back to Limen.

She cradled her baby, then put her finger in the palm of his tiny hand. He grabbed it in a vise-like grip. "I think he is going to be a weightlifter like you, Keahi."

Keahi smiled, proudly.

Masako walked around to the opposite side of the bed.

She is trying to put some space between herself and Kwon, Keahi thought.

Kwon stood across the bed from Masako, pretending to be interested in the baby, but Keahi saw his quick, fervent glances. Kwon was watching Masako, secretly.

He absolutely dislikes her but he also loves her. Poor guy.

CHAPTER THIRTEEN

Standing in front of the altar, Keahi viewed the old fisherman's black and white portrait. It was set on a small table in front of a golden statute of Buddha. The old fisherman was smiling with deep crow's feet in the corners of his wise eyes, which shone with happiness. Keahi bowed. Next to the portrait, incense rose from an urn, directly in front of Keahi, filling his nose. He almost coughed. He took a small step backwards and straightened his posture. Then he rang the altar bell and made an offering: he brought a pinch of incense to his forehead and then placed it on the smoldering incense in the urn. He bowed again. After that he sat down next to Jack and Ned on the first row of wooden benches.

Only three other persons were present; they also sat on the front row, but on the opposite side of the aisle. One of them was a *haole* woman, thin and sickly pale. She stood out garishly against the brown pews and antique-white walls of the memorial room. She had long, shiny black hair.

"I found him collapsed in his rock garden," Jack said to Keahi. "Little Chanticleer ran and got me."

Keahi looked around the almost empty room.

"Any living relatives?"

"No," Jack answered, "none that I know of. His last thoughts were about his wife. He told me that his wife and her family were all killed during the bombing raids on Tokyo during World War II."

Jack looked across the aisle at the three strangers. The pale woman turned and looked questioningly at them.

"So Ned has no living relatives?"

"I guess not. Before he died, Yukio asked me to raise him."

"Wow! That's a *huge* responsibility."

"Don't I know it."

"What was your answer?"

"That I'd look after him. And I will, for a while anyway, as long as the Social Services Department lets me. But eventually they will place him in a foster home, or a family will adopt him."

"Is that what his great-grandfather wanted?"

"No. But really, can you see me raising the boy? Look how old I am. And I'm single. And I'm not Japanese."

"I see," Keahi said, but the tone of his voice, the tone of those two words conveyed the message 'You should honor the old fisherman's wishes.'

The service was short. A priest entered the room and read a sutra, and then asked if anyone had anything to say. Jack volunteered and went up front and stood behind a lectern next to a spray of twenty green anthuriums, each the size of a small dinner plate. He said a few words, mostly for the benefit of Yukio's great-grandson, Ned. Then he sat down and hung his head in sadness. Ned cried, his head pressed against Jack's side. Jack placed his arm around Ned and held him close.

After that, the priest rang the mellow bell and called little Ned forward to offer incense on behalf of his great-grandfather. Jack helped him.

And then the priest asked if any family members were present and wanted to offer incense. The priest posed the question without an expectation that it would be answered. Consequently, the priest, and Jack and Keahi were surprised when the pale *haole* woman stood up and came forward to the altar. After making an offering of incense she returned to her seat.

The priest whisked his white *hossu* to his right, to his left, forwards and backwards. He then set it on the altar a hand's distance from the smoldering incense. Then he chanted for a few minutes. After that he said: "We look for guidance to Buddha. We look for guidance to dharma. We look for guidance to the sun god." And then the service ended and the priest slipped out a door on the side of the altar.

Keahi, Jack, and Ned stood up. Keahi stepped into the aisle and began slowly walking towards the door. Jack followed with little Ned in front. But then the pale woman cut into the aisle, blocking their way.

Her appearance frightened Ned. He turned and clung to Jack's pants leg, his small hands grasping the cotton material.

"I am his mother," the pale woman said, claiming ownership of Ned. "My name is Shelley." She made no effort to smile.

Jack was too stunned to reply. He rested his large hand on top of the boy's head and stared at the woman.

What followed was a one-way discussion about Ned's inheritance. The woman did the talking, her voice carrying throughout the quiet memorial room. She asked questions about the cottage: Did her father-in-law—Yukio—own it? What possessions did her father-in-law leave behind? Was there any money? If there was money she wanted it immediately.

Jack skillfully dodged her questions and gave no reply whatsoever.

The pale woman, frustrated, cursed him, then turned and walked briskly down the aisle. She exited the memorial viewing room.

She was already gone when they got to the front door. It was as if she had vanished.

Ned tugged at Jack's pants to get his attention and then said, "Is the ghost going to take me?"

"The ghost?" Keahi and Jack said in unison.

Jack dropped to his knees. He placed his hands on Ned's shoulders and held him firmly. He reassured him that he was safe and that the ghost was not going to take him.

Then Jack stood up. Turning to Keahi he said, "What shall I do?"

Keahi took a sharp breath. "She didn't ask about Ned. She was interested in money and property, not Ned."

"But what if she *is* the boy's mother?" Jack asked, but then he answered his own question. "I'll check her story—I'll find out who she is."

To Ned he made eye contact and said in a reflective voice: "In the meantime, Little Chanticleer, let's go home." He then affectionately rubbed Ned's hair.

Ned looked up at Jack. His eyes filled with tears. He reached out his small hand and grasped Jack's old hand, firmly. Then he took Keahi's hand, too. The three of them walked out the door together, with little Ned in the middle.

"When I can help," Keahi said, "give me a call."

"Thanks," Jack said.

Two days later, Jack called. He said he had hired a private investigator to check out the woman's story. "She's a heroin addict, a cocaine user, and a prostitute in Waikiki."

"But is she Ned's mother?"

There was silence, then the answer: "Yes, but just his biological mother."

There was another pause and Keahi surmised that Jack was controlling his emotions and collecting his thoughts.

"I've hired an attorney. He has filed the necessary papers to make me the boy's temporary guardian."

"Can you get custody?"

"He thinks so. He said it helps that Yukio named me the executor of his will. Can you believe that?"

Keahi smiled. The old fisherman was a smart guy.

"I wonder if he knew the boy's mother was alive," Jack said. He said it thoughtfully, the idea forming in his mind. "What do you think?"

"I would guess that he did. Liko said that Yukio was very upset whenever the ghost came around."

"Yes, he took the whole ghost business seriously."

"I think he knew," Keahi said.

"Yes, I do, too," Jack said. "I mean, how do you explain that your daughter-in-law is a heroin addict and a prostitute? How do you explain something like that? I guess I would have stuck with the story about the ghost, too."

"It's a good thing that Ned is scared of her," Keahi said. "He'll run and hide if she comes back."

"Yes, it all makes a lot of sense now," Jack said. "Yukio went along with the boy's story and pretended that she was a ghost to protect him."

"Do you need any help?" Keahi asked.

"I could use your truck. I need to clean out the cottage."

"Okay," Keahi said.

"And I need to haul away an old refrigerator and stove."

"I'll bring an appliance dolly."

"I'm putting his personal items in storage. Someday the boy may want them."

"Anything of value?"

"His son's medals from World War II—a Purple Heart. Some old photographs, including a wedding picture of Yukio and his wife. All the furniture—I'm going to have an auction and sell all the furniture. Use it to start a trust fund for the boy. I'm also selling the cottage and I'll put that money into the trust fund, too. The cottage is mine now, but I think that my mother would have been happy to know that I'm helping the boy."

"I thought the cottage was Yukio's?"

"No, my mother made a provision in her will that allowed Yukio to live there. But according to her will, when he passed away, the cottage reverted to me."

"And now that it's mine," Jack went on, "I've decided to sell it. I'll carry the mortgage and deposit the buyer's monthly payments into the trust fund. By the time Little Chanticleer graduates from high school, he'll have money for college."

"That's very generous of you."

"Like I said, it would have made my mother happy."

"What about the ghost?" Keahi asked.

"She gets a one-way ticket to wherever she wants. Nothing more. And I won't tell her about the boy's trust fund, either."

"Have you thought about adopting him?"

"Heaven's no! I'm not going to adopt him. I'll set up fiduciary arrangements, but I'm not going to adopt him."

"Why not?"

"For heaven's sake! He's Japanese and I'm an old *haole*."

"Well, his mother's *haole*, so he's *hapa haole*."

"Give me a break, Keahi. I'm an old man."

Later that evening, Keahi met Jack at Club Kesago, where the private investigator had said that Ned's mother hung out. Jack had asked Keahi to come with him. They both thought it ironic that Ned's mother hung out at the Captain's bar.

"It's a small island," Jack said.

"Isn't it, though."

They entered the club and paused near the front door to get oriented. After his eyes adjusted, Keahi studied the room. In the center of the club was a horseshoe-shaped bar. Barstools surrounded it. Private booths lined both sides of the walls to the right and left. Tables and chairs were pushed up against the back wall.

"I don't see her," Keahi said, looking for her ghostly presence.

"Let's ask the bartender," Jack suggested.

I doubt that asking the bartender is going to help, Keahi thought. *He won't give us the cap off a Budweiser.*

As they stepped to the bar, Keahi felt uncomfortable. Being gay, he never had occasion to visit a club where naked women sat on your lap, enticed you to buy them bottles of champagne, or danced on your tabletop for money. It was all about money and sex.

Now standing with Jack at the bar, Keahi saw a young Filipino girl dancing on a table top for a much older *haole* man, seated at a booth. Keahi watched her slowly grind her hips with her legs spread in front of the man's face. *I guess not all tourists come for our beaches.*

Two local youths nursed drinks at the bar. A young Filipino girl sat between them; her breasts were small, her nipples erect and red—either pinched recently or touched up with rouge.

The bartender slowly worked his way down the bar, serving one customer after another. He mixed a double scotch for a Japanese youth, filled a large order for a petite waitress, and finally, he stood across the wooden bar from Keahi and Jack.

Keahi's back straightened.

"What can I get you?"

"Have you seen Shelley tonight?" Jack asked.

The bartender ignored the question.

"Champagne for one of our girls?" He motioned for a woman, who was sitting at the far end of the bar near the back wall.

She shuffled across the floor, obediently, stopping beside Jack, smiling a fake smile. She brushed her hips against him as she sat down on the barstool next to him.

She had an ugly face.

"No, thanks," Jack said, "I'm just looking for Shelley."

Again the bartender ignored him.

"Have you seen Shelley?" Jack asked the girl.

The girl grasped one of Jack's legs with her knees. She threw her head backwards and her shiny, long black hair settled onto her bare back. She then leaned in towards Jack, yet sideways, placing her breasts gracefully on the top of the wooden bar, resting them so they spread out. She smiled up at Jack. "Buy me champagne?"

Her voice—sweet, yet extra sour—made Keahi shiver.

Jack looked to Keahi. His expression said, 'What now?'

Keahi rubbed his right thumb and forefinger together.

"A bottle of champagne," Jack said to the bartender. The bartender nodded, walked down to the far end of the bar, returned with a bottle, already opened.

Watered down champagne, Keahi thought. *Once you are too drunk to know the difference, they rob you with watered-down drinks.*

"That's ninety-two dollars," the bartender said.

Keahi watched as Jack paid with three fifties. "The tip is for you," Jack said to the bartender.

The bartender smiled, showing off several pointed teeth. "Sometimes she's here, sometimes she's not. Tonight she's not," he said.

"When *is* she here?" Jack asked.

"She keeps her own schedule," the bartender said. Then he turned around and started to walk away.

That reminded Keahi of how Samy had sucker punched Kwon and then turned and run away. That pissed him off.

"When was the tank pulled?" Keahi demanded, surprising himself, his voice channeling frustration and anger.

"Tank?" The bartender turned and faced Keahi. "What tank?"

"The tank that used to be in your parking lot," Keahi said.

"I don't know anything about . . . a tank."

"I heard a tank was yanked," Keahi said.

The bartender let his eyes roam up and down Keahi.

Keahi stood his ground.

Then the bartender whistled and two men stood up at a table in a corner of the room, where they had been playing Go. Keahi had not noticed them before.

Both men immediately came over. The bartender motioned towards the front door with his head. The smaller man told Keahi and Jack that it was time for them to leave.

Without any hesitation, Keahi and Jack rose from their barstools and walked out the bar. Once seated in Jack's car in the parking lot, parked directly over where the tank use to rest, Keahi said, "Looks like your investigator has more work to do."

"I'll find her," Jack said, agreeing. "I wish, though, that you hadn't said anything about the tank. This is about little Ned, not work."

"Well, asshole made me mad—taking your money and not giving you an answer. Besides, what harm did it do?"

"None, I suppose," Jack answered. "But that wasn't our business here tonight."

The explosions and Little Ned, they are both our business, Keahi thought. "Don't worry," he said. "They'll be the last ones to file a complaint."

CHAPTER FOURTEEN

S ANTOS, A LEGADO, AND THE C APTAIN'S bodyguard were seated around a large, oval table in Club Kesago, listening to the Captain vent his disapproval. There was a dark look in his eyes.

The young boy, whom Santos had first seen months ago eating a *loco moco* for breakfast at a local hotel—the same young boy who had spilled his milk into Keahi's lap—was playing with toy cars on the top of the horseshoe-shaped bar in the center of the club. He was seated on a barstool, his legs dangling far from the ground. He looked listless and was playing by himself quietly. Something seemed wrong with him, but Santos couldn't identify what it was. Something about the boy gave Santos an uneasy feeling.

"What does the Head of Department know about that tank?" the Captain shot at Santos, his voice angry.

"Nothing," Santos answered sheepishly. "He doesn't know nothing."

"Then why was he here . . . in my club . . . last night . . . asking about it?"

"I don't know," Santos said, his mind whirling, trying to think of something to say. He had never seen the Captain so mad.

The Captain turned to Alegado. "Why is he looking for this girl? What's her name?"

"I don't know," Alegado answered.

"You don't know?" the Captain asked, raising his voice.

"Not a thing."

"You, Santos, do you know this girl?"

"No." He wheezed, then added for emphasis, "I don't."

He had never seen this side of the Captain's personality, either. Unfortunately he knew nothing about this woman.

"The Head of Department comes into my club, asks about my tank, tells my bartender where the tank used to be, asks to see one of my customers, and you say 'he doesn't know nothing.'"

Santos was so unnerved that his wheezing stopped, as if his lungs had shut down altogether.

The Captain turned his penetrating eyes and scowling face back towards Alegado, who tried to maintain eye contact, but couldn't. He broke eye contact and stared down at the tabletop directly in front of him, like a child being scolded.

"I'm surrounded by idiots," the Captain said, drumming his fingers loudly on the tabletop.

"Bring the girl in," he ordered in a flat voice.

His bodyguard got up from the table and belched. He left the room through a back door that was painted black, which made it almost invisible, as if it had been strategically hidden into the back wall.

After a moment the bodyguard returned, holding a woman by her upper arm. He led her to an empty chair at the round table, directly across from the Captain.

"Sit down," the Captain ordered her.

She sat.

Santos had never seen the woman before.

The Captain pointed his cell phone at a receiver next to a large screen television mounted high on the wall and tapped the phone screen. A video played of Jack and Keahi entering his bar. She identified them, said that she had seen them at her father-in-law's funeral. Soon she was telling the Captain all about her father-in-law, the old fisherman. She explained that he had recently died and that she had met the Head of Department, Jack, at the funeral home, during the ceremony. She complained that Jack had stolen her father-in-law's money and, therefore, her son's inheritance. She complained that a lawyer had served her with papers and that Jack had filed for guardianship of her son. She said that Jack was holding her son against his will. She said that she wanted her son back.

The Captain asked a lot of questions about the boy.

Finally, when the Captain seemed satisfied with her answers, he said, "I would like to help you and your boy. Will you let me help you, Shelley?"

"Yes," she replied.

"Good. I will have my men pick up your boy and take him to my place, where he will be safe. Is this okay with you, Shelley?"

"Yes."

His eyes studied her. "You are still troubled. What else can I do for you, Shelley?"

"The inheritance," she said.

"Provide her all that she needs," the Captain ordered Alegado.

"Will you get my money for me?"

"I will give you what you need," the Captain said. The tone of his voice was stern and decisive. He was not a person that people argued with, successfully.

Shelley thanked the Captain. Santos thought she acted obsequious, fawning. He understood her motivation, though. Nothing interested her at the moment other than money for her drug habit. The Captain dismissed her and his bodyguard escorted her through the black door.

"Why is this emergency responder, Keahi, still involved with the explosion?" the Captain asked Santos.

"He shouldn't be," Santos replied. "I'm the lead in the case, ever since his partner got hurt at the pet store."

"Then explain to me why he is going around asking questions about my tank?"

"I can't," Santos said, racking his brain for an explanation, any explanation. "Maybe it has something to do with Kalele's Lab. He was involved with that too."

The Captain thought for a moment then turned to another one of his bodyguards, a Samoan who 'provided security' for many of the clubs downtown. "This emergency responder—What's his name again?" Annoyed, he turned back to Santos.

"Keahi," Santos answered.

He turned back to the bodyguard. "This emergency responder, Keahi, he needs time off. A vacation. Understand? *Wakarismasuka*?"

"*Hai*, I understand," the bodyguard replied. "I will make the necessary arrangements."

"Vacation," the Captain reiterated, "not retirement."

"*Hai*," the bodyguard replied.

Santos thought it peculiar that the Samoan said *hai* for yes. It was an obvious reflection of the loyalty that the Captain, being Japanese, demanded from his employees. *And I guess that includes me, too*, Santos thought.

"And I want the boy picked up and taken to my place at Black Point Beach," the Captain ordered.

"When?" the bodyguard asked.

"Tonight," the Captain said. "Take the boy tonight." He stood up and stretched his legs and rotated his shoulders. He had come to a decision about a bad problem and now he wanted to relax. He reached into his trousers and fondled himself, adjusting his penis and jostling his scrotum.

He walked across the club and sat down on a barstool next to the boy.

"Bring me an anise," he said to the bartender. "Then leave. Me and the boy are going to play with our toys."

The bartender brought him an anise and left through the black door. The Captain ordered everyone else to leave, too.

The boy whined. He rolled his car off the bar and it crashed onto the floor.

Santos suddenly understood that the small boy *wasn't* the Captain's grandson. Santos walked through the black door, through a small room, and then stepped into the Sunday afternoon sunshine. He felt nauseated.

He sat in his big Buick in the parking lot, wheezing, trying to catch his breath. The inside of the Buick was like an oven. He turned on the engine, powered down all the windows and cranked up the air conditioning to maximum airflow on both the passenger and the driver's side.

He glanced back towards the club and his body trembled. "This can't be happening."

He wiped the sweat off his forehead. "How am I going to get out of this shit?"

CHAPTER FIFTEEN

THE NEXT MORNING, MONDAY, Keahi stopped by Jack's office to see how things were going. Jack's secretary said he was out, and she was defensive about sharing whether he was at a meeting, was sick, or would be in later. Keahi finally gave up and returned to his cubicle. Something was wrong.

It was late morning when his phone rang.

"Someone took Ned!"

It took a long moment for that comment to register in Keahi's mind. It was Jack's voice.

"What happened?" Keahi asked.

"I'm at the police station." Jack cleared his throat. "They haven't helped at all."

"What can I do?"

There was a pause. "Meet me at the Coffee Stop on Ward Avenue." Jack's voice cracked. "I'm going to grab a cup and then go back home. I need to look around the cottage again. I'll be at the Stop in five minutes."

"I'll be there," Keahi said, and Jack hung up.

The Coffee Stop on Ward Avenue was not a drive-through, but it was next to Sports Authority, so it had ample parking and was easy to get in and out of quickly, even during lunch hour traffic. Keahi arrived before Jack and got them both a place in line. When Jack arrived, he joined Keahi near the front of the line, oblivious to the stink eye drilling into the back of his head. He was too preoccupied.

"What happened?" Keahi asked.

"He disappeared. I woke up and he was gone." Jack turned, looked at the people in the line behind him, saw them frowning at him—didn't care—and then turned back to Keahi again. "Someone took him. Someone came into the house last night and took him."

"His mother?"

"Maybe. I called the police. They searched the house, the cottage, and the beach. They even brought in a police dog and a rescue helicopter."

"Did they find anything?"

"No, not a trace. Nothing."

"Could he have gone to the beach?"

"No, he wouldn't leave the yard, not unless someone forced him. He's too afraid of the ghost."

Keahi nodded, recalling how frightened Ned had been during the funeral.

They reached the cash register and a young boy took Keahi's order: a tall coffee and a local fish plate—rice, macaroni salad, mahi-mahi burger. Jack ordered two small codfish sandwiches and a large Coke. They sat down across from each other at a small, inside table.

Absentmindedly, Jack unwrapped one of his breaded fish sandwiches, removing the blue paper and setting it on his plastic tray. Tartar sauce ran out the sides of the bun. He globbed it down.

"What happened at the police station?"

"Nothing. I filled out paperwork. Gave them Ned's picture."

"Did you tell them about Shelley?"

"Yes."

"What did they say?"

"Nothing." Jack opened the second fish sandwich, took a few fast bites of the deep-fried fish, and then returned the sandwich to the blue wrapper. He crumpled the half-eaten sandwich and the wrapper into a tight ball, dropping it onto his plastic food tray. "Her police record is confidential."

He laughed nervously. Keahi noted the fear clinching his jaw. Jack rested his elbows on the table. With his hands cupped together and his thumbs supporting his chin, he stared down at the blue ball on the plastic tray.

Good Lord, Keahi thought.

Jack cleared his voice. "Dog food," he said, losing his composure.

They both laughed, nervously.

"I'm going back home to check around the property again."

Keahi nodded approval.

Keahi decided not to join the search effort. If the police dogs had been unable to sniff out the boy, Keahi doubted that his own presence would make a difference. So Keahi went to work as usual, except that he kept his phone line open in case Jack called.

He was unable to concentrate on his current cases, so he straightened the papers on his desk instead, and then started cleaning out the old cases in his file cabinet. Soon he had filled a monster-sized recycling container, which was another one of Jack's initiatives. He tilted the heavy green container onto its big back wheels and pushed it through the office to the elevator. When he reached the basement, he wheeled the container into the recycling room, where he ran into Santos. It was a bad day, indeed.

Santos was smashing cans and tossing them into an open cardboard container that had RECYCLED CANS ONLY in large red letters on its side.

"Damn idiots," Santos said. "Why don't they crush their cans?"

"Ned is missing," Keahi announced.

"Who's Ned?" Santos replied in an irritated voice, deciding not to even acknowledge the existence of Ned.

He smashed another can under his steel plated, steel-toed boots just as a roach crawled out. Roach guts spread out on the aluminum can and the floor. "Damned roaches," Santos mumbled, trying to control his mounting fear. "They're everywhere."

Santos stopped and stared at Keahi.

"Why are you staring at me?" Keahi asked.

Santos almost unburdened himself. He almost told Keahi about the lab arson, about the Captain's sexual abuse of small boys, about the Captain kidnapping Ned, and that the Captain had ordered Keahi to be beaten. But he didn't because he was now terrified of the Captain.

"Rinse your damned cans!"

"What?"

"You heard me. I'm telling you: You had better start rinsing your damned cans!"

Keahi parked the recycling container, then turned and walked away, disgusted at Santos's sudden outburst. He didn't know what was bothering Santos, but he wanted no part of it. He had enough worries of his own. He stepped to the elevator and pushed the 'up' button.

He's a mess, Keahi thought.

CHAPTER SIXTEEN

PUMPING UP IN THE GYM WAS KEAHI'S way of dealing with stress; consequently, for the last few months his workouts had become intense, strenuous and lasted an hour and a half or longer. Lately, when he left the gym he was physically exhausted, but his mind was clearer and more at peace.

Tonight, Keahi started his workout with a warm-up on the stationary bike. As his legs cycled round and round he thought about Liko, Toi, Santos, Kwon, Ned, Lim's newborn, drownings, explosions, and even love. He felt his legs begin to tighten. And who had abducted Ned?

As his anger mixed with frustration, he decided to pound his legs, so he moved to the leg extension machine and continued his warm-up. First 25 leg extensions at 80 pounds each. Next 12 repetitions at 150 pounds. Then 10 reps at 300, the machine's maximum.

When his thighs were burning and his heart was warmed up and his mind was ready, he walked over to the leg press. He piled on the Olympic weight plates and stepped underneath the bar. The cool metal felt good on his shoulders. He lifted the tremendous weight off the rack using his legs. His legs were much stronger than the rest of his body, and the weight he could bear on his shoulders was just slightly less.

Balancing the heavy bar on his shoulders, he took two steps backward, clearing himself from the squat rack and the protection it provided in case his legs crumpled. But he didn't want the protection. Not tonight. He felt the adrenaline flowing through his arteries and into his legs.

He set his feet at shoulder width, straightened his back and gazed upwards, towards the ceiling and the bright fluorescent lights. He slightly bent his knees. Then he lowered himself until his thighs were parallel to the floor. His feet stayed flat. There was no wobble. Neither his toes nor his heels came up off the floor. Then he raised the bar back up in a smooth, controlled motion.

He did another seven reps, and then he returned the bar to the rack and added more weight. After two more sets, he did leg presses followed by calf raises, both sitting and standing.

Then he pushed himself through an exceptionally painful series of abdominal exercises, including crunches.

After that, he returned to the exercise cycle for a 60-minute cardio workout. He felt the remaining energy drain from his body as he biked up and down imaginary mountain paths.

Keahi walked down the wide sidewalk, heading towards Diamond Head, amazed at how bustling Waikiki was even at ten o'clock at night. He could barely walk, thanks to his strenuous workout, but his mind was at peace.

He gazed at the ocean and then he surveyed the beach. Now that the cleanup was winding down, he expected things at work would fall back into a normal, bureaucratic routine. For the moment, he refused to entertain such a depressing idea. Instead, he stubbornly protected his hard-gained peace of mind.

His immediate goal was to go home, shower, and meet Angelica and Carol at their place, as he had promised them. Together they would watch the fireworks that would usher in the New Year.

"Hello babu," he said aloud, his voice filled with veneration as he passed the statue of Gandhi. "I hope you had a merry Christmas and I wish you a happy New Year."

He passed the entrance to the zoo, crossed Monsarrat Street and started across the bandstand area.

He had overexerted himself at the gym and was exhausted. The last time he had pushed his body this hard was when his lover Daniel had died. His grief had been inconsolable, and it was still inconsolable.

He was so tired. He wondered whether he could make it across the park without stopping to rest. And he would have stopped to rest, but he was unsure if he would be able to motivate his aching body to start again, to finish the half-mile home.

Where did my youth go?

He passed a shallow man-made pond.

Perhaps I'll call Angelica and Carol and cancel.

He walked parallel to tall hedge of mock orange that grew along the chain link fence enclosing the backside of what used to be the Kodak Hula Show area.

And then he felt a sharp pain in his right side. He whirled around.

A man was holding a knife.

Keahi pressed his hand just below his ribs—felt wetness flowing between his fingers.

"Why?" he asked, astonished.

He felt warm blood flowing over the back of his hand, a steady stream of blood pulsing out of his side. "What's the matter with you?"

He backed up to the mock orange hedge. He heard the branches rustle, branches scraping against chain link. And then he felt a blow to the back of his head.

His fatigued legs gave out and he dropped to his knees.

The man in front of him with the knife approached cautiously. Keahi didn't move. The pain in his side was excruciating. He didn't want to bend at the waist. He didn't want to try to stand up. He decided to stay on his knees.

Above and behind Keahi, a second man bent over him. A pierced nose. A pierced eyebrow. Shiny metal studs. Keahi saw a necklace fall out from his shirt. It dangled in the air in front of his chest. No, it was a woman's chest! Small childlike breasts. So young. Fourteen? Maybe fifteen? And the pendant? An animal? A hyena? A golden hyena?

"I have nothing of value," Keahi said to her.

She kicked him in the head and he fell onto his side.

Then he saw the toe of her boot coming straight at his face.

He woke up to the sound of a loud bang.

At first he thought that he was in the child care playground, lying with his face in the grass.

Then he heard more bangs.

Firecrackers?

Then he remembered that he had been attacked.

The rolling sound of thousands of explosions told him that it was midnight, that the fireworks had begun, that the people on Oahu were ushering in a New Year.

That meant at least two hours had passed. He had been lying in Kapiolani Park, motionless, for two hours. He wondered if people had walked by him, thinking that he was asleep or passed out, just another homeless person.

He thought of the knife wound. *Am I going to die? All alone? Like this?*

He listened to the intermittent explosions of firecrackers in the distance. Acrid smoke drifted over the park, settled, enveloped him.

Then he heard a siren. He hoped it was an ambulance coming for him, but then he realized that it was a fire engine. He recalled someone saying that it was too dry for fireworks.

Illegal bottle rockets streaked across the sky and exploded in little bursts of white flame with loud bangs. An illegal artillery firework exploded with a tremendous boom!

Oahu was burning and choking.

He slowly became aware that his arm was asleep. It ached. He had fallen on it and he was now lying on it. He wanted to move it but couldn't. He wanted to roll over, but couldn't. And then he realized, suddenly, that he had fallen on the hand that was pressed against his side. It was pressing against the wound in his side, the knife wound.

Do I have to save myself? he wondered.

And then he lost consciousness.

CHAPTER SEVENTEEN

IT RETURNED AS HE AWOKE, a feeling that his life was over. Last night a man and a girl had attacked him, and he had lain in the grass near the bandstand in Kapiolani Park with a knife wound in his side and a gash across his forehead. He had lain in the grass face down, listening to millions of firecrackers and shrouded in acrid smoke. Roaches had crawled over his body. The grass was alive with roaches! He had watched them crawling across the sharp tips of the grass.

And as he had lain there, unable to move or yell for help, lying in the wet grass where blood had pumped out of his side, he had thought about dying—and the possibility mortified him. It mortified him because he saw clearly that he had wasted the most valuable years of his life: he had spent the prime of his life sitting in a cubicle, wasting valuable days, valuable hours. And without even a window!

What foolishness! I could have been a performer, a singer a dancer. Not a bureaucrat!

Later, as the first sunlight appeared, someone had approached him and then a small group of people had gathered around. Someone had poked him with the end of a rolled-up grass mat: "Maybe he's dead."

Then ambulance workers had arrived, and it took three of them to move him from the grass onto a stretcher.

When they hoisted him into the air, one of them had said: "I don't think this guy's homeless. He's wearing gym clothes."

His partner had responded: "I don't care brah, just don't drop your end. Don't make me pick him up again."

They had carried him on a stretcher across the grass to an asphalt parking lot where they had lowered the gurney's wheels. Then they had rolled him on uneven asphalt to the ambulance. It had been bumpy and jarring. And each time that he was jostled, he had felt acute pain in his side.

Why are they treating me so carelessly?

When he next awoke, he was in a hospital bed, alone. Again, he reflected on the embarrassment that he had felt believing that he had been left to die.

He lay in the hospital bed feeling sorry for himself and his wasted years, painfully acknowledging that his youth and middle years were past, that his strengths and talents were undeveloped and unused and, consequently, that his current life was one of mediocrity, of bureaucracy, of lost opportunities.

Then a nurse gave him a sponge bath.

That was also embarrassing.

"How long have I been asleep?"

"Three days. Four nights."

"Really?" He thought only one night had passed.

"You have a nasty wound in your side and a deep cut on your head. And you lost a lot of blood."

"Am I going to be okay?"

"Your doctor is making her morning rounds; she can answer your questions. But I can tell you this: you are lucky to be alive. That's what I've heard. You are lucky to be alive."

After the nurse left he drifted back to sleep.

When he awoke again, the nurse was again at his side, holding his arm, checking the tape and gauze pad on a needle that had been inserted into a vein on the top of his hand.

"You had visitors. Two pretty girls."

The nurse told him that the girls—one blonde, one Chinese—had stayed by his bedside the first day and most of the first night until the doctor had ordered them to go home and get some rest. The nurse said the two pretty girls had taken turns at his bedside the next two days, watching over him.

"What time is it?"

"Four-thirty."

"Morning or night?"

"Morning."

"No wonder it's so quiet."

"Another pretty girl left this for you." The nurse handed Keahi a small envelope. "She was Japanese. Very nice."

He opened it. His hands shook. Just opening and holding the card was an effort.

It was a New Year's card, with a handwritten note: *Sorry to hear of your injuries. Hope you get a handsome male nurse. Get well soon. Masako.*

Keahi smiled.

He hoped she would visit again, soon. He recalled how comforting it had been when the team had gotten together after the oil spill to crack a few beers. Now, he wanted to see them again.

The first to return were Angelica and Carol. They arrived shortly after the sun rose and filled Keahi's room with the glow of morning light.

"Hey, how are you?" Carol asked.

"I'll be fine, once I get the hang of the bedpan," Keahi joked, trying to set a light tone. He smiled for them.

From the foot of the bed, Carol reacted by reaching over the bed rail and grabbing his big toe, which was under the white bed sheet.

"Hey," Keahi said, "I guess I haven't told you in a while."

"Told me what?" Carol said, holding his big toe.

"That I love you," he said, grinning.

"Someone should knock you on the head more often," Angelica said, playing with a curly tuft of black hair that stuck out of the white bandage wrapped around his head.

"I love you too, Angelica," he said.

Carol twisted Keahi's toe, gently. "Who did this to you?"

"A man and a kid," Keahi replied. "Can you believe that? A young girl kicked me in the face."

"Local?"

"Yeah, they talked pidgin."

Carol gently bent his big toe.

"What are you doing with my toe? You got a foot fetish now?"

Carol laughed and then popped the big knuckle.

Masako dropped in later in the morning wearing a new dress: a bright, strapless print gown. She radiated fuchsia. Keahi felt warmed by the large flowery print. Flowery mumus always gave him a feeling of comfort.

"I redo my wardrobe every New Year's," she confided. "And I've decided to forgive Kwon."

"Why's that?"

"It's a Japanese tradition." She smiled and her upper white teeth showed. "Wouldn't he just hate that? I mean, me forgiving him because it's the *Japanese* thing to do?"

Keahi thought it was both funny and ironic. He loved her for it.

"But please don't tell him," she said, resting her hand on his shoulder. "I want it to be our secret."

He looked at Masako, trying to find the right words to tell her how Kwon felt about her. Finally he said it as simply as he could. "He loves you, you know."

"All my boyfriends love me." She gently squeezed his shoulder. "Why would he be any different? Next thing I know, he'll start stalking me."

There was a pause and then she quickly added, "If he does, I'll take out a temporary restraining order." Her mood changed from happy to pensive, as quickly as the morning sun had slipped behind the curtains.

The rest of the core team—Lim, Toi, and Kwon—dropped in shortly after Masako left. When they saw him, they were appalled by how badly he had been beaten.

"Thought you would want to see this," Lim said. He handed Keahi the morning edition of the paper, folded to a few paragraphs about the assault. Lying flat on his back, Keahi held the newspaper over his face. He read the short piece and then studied the sketch of the girl who had attacked him. The sketch was a very good likeness of her; it captured the anger in her eyes and her disenfranchised attitude. And the article described her gold hyena necklace. Surely someone would recognize her picture or remember such a distinctive necklace.

"That's her," Keahi said. "The police artist got it right. We worked on it yesterday afternoon."

Kwon picked up Keahi's medical chart hanging on the foot of his bed. "Megadoses of penicillin, huh?"

"And painkillers," Keahi said, smiling.

"Even a small dose of penicillin would kill me," Kwon said. "It affects the toxicity of one of my arthritis drugs."

"We miss you back at the office," Lim said to Keahi.

Keahi nodded with a smile, recognizing Lim for his obligatory hospital visit and comment.

They chatted a while longer and then everyone left, except for Toi. Once they were alone, she adjusted Keahi's bed sheets around his upper body, smoothing out the wrinkles. Then she placed her small hand gently on his forehead.

"If you need anything at all," Toi offered. "Someone to talk to, anything. I'm here."

Keahi said nothing.

"I know how you feel," Toi added.

"How's that?"

"Small," Toi said. "Very small."

Keahi stared at her. *Yes, I am feeling small. Very small.* He nodded.

In the late afternoon, Keahi's great-aunt paid him a visit. She leaned over the side bed rails—standing on her tiptoes—and gave him a kiss on both cheeks and then firmly grasped his hand in a comforting way. He could feel both her age and her strength through her small hands. Her pikaki perfume filled the hospital room, displacing the smell of disinfectants. Keahi was grateful for that.

A feeling of embarrassment overwhelmed him and he broke into tears. It was the same feeling of embarrassment he had felt when he was lying in the park, helpless.

"There was a moment when I thought I was going to die. And I felt so embarrassed! I kept asking myself, how did I let this happen? How did it happen?"

"It wasn't your fault," his great-aunt said. "You shouldn't blame yourself for being mugged."

"No, no. I'm not embarrassed about that. I'm ashamed that I have wasted my *life*! I could have done so much more. But look at me. I'm a bureaucrat! For God's sake! A mediocre bureaucrat!"

"I've been telling you that for years, Keahi." She patted his hand as she admonished him. "And now you finally understand?"

"Yes. I do understand. And I am so embarrassed. I have settled for so little." He looked into her eyes. "I used to have dreams."

She smiled at him.

"I wanted to dance, to chant . . . and now look at me."

She gently squeezed his hand.

He suddenly realized the depth of her understanding. She understood his desire to sing, to dance, to perform. And she also understood his continuing grief over the loss of Daniel. Yes, she knew all about Daniel, too.

He now recalled how he had taken the office job to pay for Daniel's home care and, after that, to pay off Daniel's medical bills. Yes, he had been responsible and good. He smiled. But then he had become complacent, lazy. His smile turned to a frown. In fact, after the bills were paid off, he should have returned to his performing! *Why didn't I?*

"My god, Auntie! I have buried myself in a cubicle! I have a monthly paycheck, a retirement plan, 21 days of vacation per year, a nice place to live. But—"

"It's not enough," she said, finishing his sentence.

"Yes! So much is missing!"

"Most government jobs are like that, Keahi."

"I could have done so much more with my life." The tears rolled down his face. "I am so embarrassed. I thought I was going to die, and before I had even lived!"

"So tell me, Keahi." She was holding his hand tightly. "What are you going to do, now?"

"I don't know. I really don't know."

"But you have been doing *that* for years!" she chided.

CHAPTER EIGHTEEN

Santos saw little Ned aboard the Captain's boat. He recognized the boy from the lawn bowling party at Jack's cottage a few months earlier. He hadn't talked to the boy that day, but he was sure that it was him. The boy was seated in a deck chair next to an older boy who held a toy truck in his lap. Santos thought both boys looked listless and sad.

"Is that the woman's son?" Santos asked the Captain.

"Yes."

The Captain turned in the direction of the boys and called them to come. The older boy immediately climbed out of his chair, set his toy truck in the seat, and came to the Captain's side, heeling like a puppy. The fisherman's great-grandson, however, remained seated. It seemed to Santos that little Ned was now watching the Captain, quietly, like a cat watching a mean dog. The boy's eyes were so intently focused on the Captain that Santos imagined the hair on Ned's neck was standing up, just like the hair on an alert cat.

"Why aren't you playing with your new friend?"

"I don't like him," the older boy answered.

The Captain frowned and ordered both boys below deck. Santos watched them disappear down a flight of stairs to the lower deck.

The Captain lit a marijuana cigarette, took a few puffs, and passed it to Santos.

Santos held the cigarette out to his side, letting the smoke drift away. He didn't like the effects of marijuana, the way it altered his perception of time, the way it slowed everything down. It made him paranoid. So he passed the cigarette back to the Captain.

"Still don't smoke?"

"No."

"That's too bad." The Captain shook his head. "It's relaxing."

"But you don't know what's in that stuff," Santos said.

"This is the highest quality." The Captain put the cigarette between his lips and inhaled deeply. A long ash fell.

"Ah! The sharks have appeared," he said. "I have a surprise for you, Santos."

Santos glanced out in the direction of the Captain's gaze. He saw a perforated bucket trailing behind the boat. From the churning school of fish around it, he guessed that it contained offal and other bloody animal parts.

A few minutes later, a girl was brought on deck. Santos instantly recognized her as the girl in the newspaper: she looked just like the police artist's sketch. "She's the girl that attacked Keahi."

The Captain nodded. "That's too bad. If you can recognize her, anyone can."

Santos saw that she was wearing the gold hyena pendant that had been described in the newspaper article. He wondered why she would wear something like that.

A large Samoan brought the girl before them and forced her down on her knees. Her hands were behind her back and tied at the wrists.

"What are we going to do?" the Captain asked the girl.

She didn't answer. She just stared up at the Captain.

"We can't let you get picked up by the police. Can we?"

The girl remained quiet.

"Of course we can't," the Captain replied for her.

"What do you think we should do, Santos?"

Santos thought of the sharks attracted to the bloody offal. He looked at the girl. She seemed to be in a state of shock, like a mouse pinned under the paw of a big cat. He looked back at the Captain. "Send her to Thailand . . . some place like that."

"But how can I get you off the island?" the Captain asked the girl.

"I don't want to leave," she said. "Let me stay. Let me work for you."

"Ah, but that is the problem. How can you work for me if you are in Thailand? And if you can't work for me, why should I pay for an airline ticket, run the risk that someone at the airport will recognize you?" He shook his head. "And even if they don't, I'd have to give you money to resettle."

He shook his head again. "You see, you are a liability—an expensive liability."

"I want to work for you," the girl repeated.

"Free her hands," the Captain ordered the big Samoan. The Samoan reached down and hoisted the girl to her feet. Then Santos saw the flash of a knife and the girl's hands fell to her sides.

"I can stay here," the girl said.

"What? On my boat?"

"At your house. I can work for you."

"Idiots!" The Captain's voice was angry. "I'm surrounded by idiots."

He lurched forward as if he was going to strike the girl.

She flinched.

He took a step back.

"Do you think I would harbor a fugitive in my house? Do you think I am stupid?"

Santos looked at the girl. Her body began to tremble.

"Do you think that I would take a doped-up bitch like you into my house?"

Again the Captain lurched forward into the girl's personal space.

She cringed.

Again he stepped back.

"Do you think I could trust you?"

The Captain rocked forward on his toes, turned his head slightly to the side, flashed a small, toothy smile. Then he rocked backwards. He reached into his pocket and took out another marijuana cigarette. He lit it and puffed it.

"Would you like a smoke?"

"Yes," she replied.

He passed her the cigarette. But her hands were trembling so badly that she dropped it onto the deck. And wind blew it overboard. It disappeared into the ocean.

Santos looked on with mingled surprise and fear. He watched as the Captain nonchalantly reached beneath his aloha shirt, which was hanging loosely, and produced a .357 Mag with a shiny barrel.

He held it out to Santos: "Shoot her."

The big Samoan stepped out from behind the girl.

The Captain placed the handle of the gun in Santos's hand.

It's heavy, Santos thought, staring at the gun. It had a long barrel. He looked back at the Captain.

"Now," ordered the Captain. "Aim the gun at the bitch and pull the trigger."

Santos's jaw dropped. "What?"

"Pull the trigger."

Santos looked again at the gun in his hand. He noticed that the end of the long barrel was now shaking. And then he realized that his hand and even his whole arm was shaking. Suddenly the gun was much heavier than just a moment ago.

He looked from the gun to the girl. As their eyes met, she bolted. She jumped over the railing into the water. She started swimming away from the boat.

The big Samoan grabbed a nearby life jacket and threw it in her direction. It sailed out in front of her, directly in her path. She swam to it, grabbed it, tucked it under her. And then she started swimming even harder, away from the boat.

"Nice touch." The Captain laughed.

"Thanks boss," the Samoan responded. He smiled, too.

Santos looked from the Samoan to the Captain. He couldn't believe what he had just seen and heard.

"No!" the girl yelled.

Santos glanced back in her direction. He saw the sharks.

He watched the girl turn and start swimming back to the boat. But the sharks cut her off. They circled her. They swam closer and closer. Santos's jaw dropped. A shark attacked and grabbed the life jacket and swam off with it. The girl shrieked a shrill note that sent shivers down his spine. Shocked, Santos turned away.

The Captain reached into his shirt pocket and retrieved another ganja cigarette, lit it and said, "Sure you don't want a smoke?"

Santos's throat constricted. He was unable to answer. Instead, he shook his head. He passed the gun back to the Captain.

"I'm hungry," the Captain said. "Let's collect some shark fins. What do you say, Santos?"

At the Captain's direction, the big Samoan was soon gaffing sharks and pulling them aboard. The Captain slashed off their fins, which he dropped into a beige colored plastic bucket, and then the Samoan threw the maimed sharks back into the ocean.

Occasionally the water boiled with a feeding frenzy, as one of the maimed sharks was attacked and then devoured by its brethren.

The big Samoan retrieved the shredded life jacket, which had floated back to the boat.

Santos now glanced at the area where he had seen the sharks and the girl. The ocean there was now quiet.

A fourteen-foot tiger shark appeared. The Captain watched it in stoned admiration.

"It's been a good day!" the Captain said.

He smiled at Santos, then added, "Wish I had caught a megamouth, though."

A shiver passed through Santos's body. He had no idea what a megamouth was, but it sounded bad.

They sailed back to the harbor and the Yacht Club.

PART FOUR
RESOLUTION

CHAPTER NINETEEN

AFTER A WEEK IN THE HOSPITAL, Keahi returned home in a wheelchair, which the doctors said he would have to use because of his closed head injury. He still had mild headaches and dizziness. He slipped his hand beneath his aloha shirt and ran it gently along the ragged twelve-inch incision, now stapled. The surgeon had removed not only his kidney but also a rib. The knife wound had been vicious.

When he entered his studio, he was astonished to find that Angelica and Carol had used his spare key to enter. They had thoroughly cleaned his dishes, the bathroom, and changed his bedding. And they had filled his refrigerator shelves with enough prepared food for a week. His eyes welled up with tears.

He confined himself to the wheelchair and limited his physical activities to watching television and listening to music. But he still had dizzy spills; while seated in the wheelchair he would suddenly become lightheaded and anxious and his pulse would start racing.

Is this my life from now on?

Keahi groaned as the wheelchair rolled over several large, uneven breaks in the sidewalk that ran alongside the elementary school next door to his apartment. Then he and Toi crossed at the traffic light. A motorist making a fast right turn almost failed to see him. The motorist braked and her sport utility vehicle skidded and stopped slightly sideways with its bumper an inch from Keahi's wheelchair. Keahi backed up and made eye contact with her over the hood of the overbearing SUV. He gave her the meanest stink eye he could muster, and yelled, "Get that gas-guzzling over-sized piece of shit off the road!" In response, the short driver revved her V8 engine and peeled off, leaving Keahi shrouded in black smoke from her screeching tires. The smell of burnt rubber infuriated him.

He looked at Toi. Her mouth was wide open, her jaw dropped. He wondered if she was shocked that he was almost hit by an SUV, or by his anger at the driver. She was surprised by both, he decided.

Once across the street, they cut across the grass to the center of the park. Now the ride was bumpy, but the wheelchair rolled across the dry, short tufts of grass without difficulty. The overused fields were as hard as pavement.

Then Keahi watched as Toi unwrapped and assembled a new kite she had brought as a get well present. The kite's red nylon carrying sack doubled as its tail, which she tied onto its yellow, red and orange body. He was delighted.

She tied a spool of string to the kite, handed him the spool, and then paced off 20 feet. Holding the kite in front of her, she ordered, "Pull it into the air." He pulled and kept tension in the string and the trade winds caught the kite and it shot into the air.

She walked over and sat on the grass next to him. She frowned. "How come you get the chair?"

He smiled, understanding that she was teasing him. "Lucky, I guess."

She returned his smile and for the first time in weeks he felt relaxed. He fed the kite string, let it soar, reeled it in. He watched the tail of the kite flapping in the trade winds. He let the colorful kite out again.

"I can't believe that I was attacked—here in this park, over there, by that fence line." He nodded toward Waikiki.

"Yes," Toi responded, "and I find it hard to believe that Hanauma Bay was destroyed."

Keahi shook his head. "My memories of the attack are high definition. And I can remember the smells, too."

"Like a scratch and sniff picture?" Toi suggested.

"Yes. I remember the smell of dry grass and the stink of firecrackers."

And then the words came and he described what he had thought and felt. He talked and talked and talked. And she listened, which pleased him. And he appreciated the fact that she was careful not to interrupt, not to dominate, not to lead him.

After that, they reeled in the kite.

Then they found shade under one of the large baobab trees along the side of the park on Leahi Street.

He scratched through the detritus beneath the tree with the edge of his slipper. "What do you believe in?"

She stared at him but did not answer.

"Please, I would like to know."

He sat patiently through a long moment of silence.

Finally she said, "I believe that the forces of nature are much more powerful than we are. I believe that nature can and will rebound when we challenge her, no matter what we throw at her—we aren't as all-powerful as we like to think. Nature *will* rebound. Perhaps not in a way we can foresee, or even in a way that will please us, but nature will always continue. That is what I have learned, and that is what gives me comfort. Nature will continue despite us."

"Do you fear death?" he asked.

"I do, but I understand it better now. I've witnessed death twice. Once at Hanauma Bay when all the marine life perished. Before that, on a ship between Vietnam and Thailand."

"What was it like growing up in Vietnam?"

"It was not easy. The kids called me *bui doi*, 'dust of life'. *An my den*, black American. *My lai*, American mix."

"I'm sorry," Keahi said.

"It's okay. I've thought about it a lot. You know, because I had no father, I had no future in Vietnam. You see, in Vietnam, the father *is* the household, and patriarchy is strictly observed. But my father had left Vietnam and returned to America."

Keahi made eye contact, then asked: "Will you share your story with me? Please?"

Keahi felt Toi studying him, sizing him up, so to speak. Then she nodded her head, yes.

"After the war, it got worse. My mother and I were singled out. We had a small apartment until the government seized it. Then we were told to move to the countryside. We were fortunate because we were given shelter in a small village by an elderly Chinese couple."

"I awoke one morning and my mother was dead. I don't know what caused her death. Maybe a stroke, maybe a heart attack. I don't know. I was very fortunate because the Chinese couple were kind. If they had not been good people, I am sure my life would have ended tragically, long ago."

"It was in 1980 that we escaped Vietnam. That was shortly after the Chinese invaded, and my adoptive parents, who were Chinese, had to flee to escape persecution in the village. They had lived for generations in that village, but their Vietnamese neighbors still persecuted them. My Chinese parents and I, and many other people, crowded aboard a leaky boat, all of us risking our lives for a dream. My Chinese parents' dream was for peace and security. My dream was to find my father."

"I will never forget their kindness. You see, they did not have to take me with them. In fact, it was very expensive. And I was a liability."

"When we left Vietnam, we were all scared. Even I had heard the stories about sea pirates—women raped, all of your stuff stolen, men thrown overboard and left behind to drown. And that was our fate, too. My Chinese parents were murdered."

"Of all the women on our boat, only I escaped being raped. I jumped overboard into an ocean filled with sharks.

Yes, I saw the sharks and to this day I do not know why they did not attack me. They did eat others. Many were less fortunate than I. The pirates threw them off the boat for sport."

"When I arrived—it was Malaysia, not Thailand—my troubles truly began. I lived in a squalid refugee camp for two long years. It was terrible. Most of the people in my camp were well-educated, or had been farmers, or at one time had been successful storekeepers, but in the camp we were treated as if we were nothing."

"Oh, my!" Toi sighed. "I apologize for rambling on and on and doing all the talking. I guess I got off the point of my story, which was to tell you this: It was when I was in the water with the sharks, when I faced the possibility of death, that I learned how quickly a life can end. As quick as you can snap your fingers." She snapped her fingers. "That is how quick your life can end."

"Yes," Keahi said, breaking his silence. He had been attentive to her every word. "I, too, understand that now."

They continued to talk for a long time about many different things, including the changes in Hawaii because of the oil spill: crime was increasing, especially violent crime. Hawaii had always had problems with theft, but now Hawaii was seeing a marked increase in violent crimes, including murders. It was alarming. And it seemed directly related to the oil spill in some way.

At one point Keahi said, "Maybe Lim is right. Maybe we should leave?"

Toi had no answer. All she could do was shake her head and share his disbelief.

At the end of the afternoon, she pushed him back to his apartment building and helped him climb the three flights of steps to his studio. He watched anxiously as she carried his wheelchair back up the stairs.

After a while, she said goodbye. She left the kite as a gift.

After she left, he thought about her. She seemed to be recovering. And then he realized that neither of them had talked about Liko. For his part, he was now glad that Toi was involved with Liko, although he wasn't sure exactly what their relationship was. He suddenly realized, too, that she had chosen to discuss the things that were important to him: the mugging, his sudden mortality, his thoughts about life and death.

Later, he called the mayor's office and complained about the condition of the sidewalk by the school.

Then he sat on his lanai, drinking Foster's until he nearly passed out. His remaining kidney nearly burst.

"You're pulling my leg?" Toi said. They were watching a tortoise chew its leafy dinner.

"No, I'm not," Keahi answered. "I've never been to the zoo until now."

"But you live here!"

"So what? I know someone who was born on Molokai and has never visited the leper colony."

"No!"

"I even know someone at work who has never snorkeled Hanauma Bay."

"Who's that?"

"Pete."

"No way!"

"I'm serious," Keahi said. "He told me himself. He has never gotten his feet wet in Hanauma Bay."

"How can you go through life without exploring your own backyard?"

Keahi thought, *It's easy. You just sit in a cubicle in a dull office building. Or you spend your evenings watching television. Or you sit on your lanai drinking beer until you pass out.*

Toi took his arm. He was no longer using a wheelchair. "I'll show you something that will cheer you up."

"What's that?"

"African hunting dogs," she said. "A pack of wild dogs, right here in your own backyard."

At first glance the dogs looked like hyenas. They had the characteristic large head and the mottled coat of fur: dark black softened by yellow, white and tan.

"They look funny." Keahi marveled at their long, slender legs; their big, black muzzles; their large, erect, round ears. And their tails were as long as their body and had white tufts of hair on the end.

"A female and two males," Toi told him. "I heard that she is pregnant again."

"The animal handlers must be excited," Keahi said.

"No doubt about *that*," Toi replied. "Imagine coming into work and having a litter of wild puppies to play with—a half dozen balls of fur with big ears and sharp teeth and long legs."

"Yeah, big furry heads with sharp teeth."

They watched the wild dogs for a long time, then as they walked to the next exhibit, Keahi said, "I've been thinking about changing jobs, finding something different."

"Like what?"

"Something other than a government job."

"In Hawaii?" The tone of Toi's voice conveyed disbelief. "Like what?"

"I don't know," Keahi answered, a bit defensively. "What would *you* do if you changed jobs?"

"Go back to school. Do some research."

"A Ph.D.?"

"Yes, in human evolution."

Keahi gave her a quizzical look.

"I've always suspected that somewhere in our evolutionary past, we returned to the water."

"That we evolved from fish?"

"No, no. That we are descended from primates that later returned to the water for a while."

"Why do you think that?"

"You won't laugh if I tell you?"

"Me? Laugh? Hey, I'm hurting here. I won't laugh at anyone who will share their wisdom with me."

"Well, it's more of a feeling. It's not based on anything scientific. Sometimes I have such a strong attraction to the ocean, such strong feelings towards ocean life—and not just the whales and dolphins and monk seals, but *all* life in the ocean—that I believe we must have returned to the water sometime during our evolution."

"I'm not sure I understand."

"Okay, let me explain," Toi said. "I believe that while we were still primates, before we became human, we became intimately acquainted with water again, long enough to change our bodies and our minds. I believe that is the primary reason many of us are strongly attracted to water."

"Is there any proof to support your idea?"

"It's not an original idea," Toi said. "I wish it was my idea, but it's not. However, I do think that I could find an original way to put the hypothesis to the test."

They hunted for a bench, and when they found one across from the elephant exhibit, they sat down.

"What if your hypothesis is proven wrong?"

She shrugged her shoulders. "Our evolutionary past is past. But who knows what the future holds! The future is wonderfully pregnant with possibilities. It is impossible for us to stay as we are. Evolution is changing us."

"But will the change be for the better?" Keahi asked.

"I hope so," Toi said.

Then she smiled. "So what do you want to do, Keahi?"

"I'm searching, I'm looking, I'm thinking. As soon as I find it," Keahi said, "I'll share it with you."

CHAPTER TWENTY

IT WAS A BEAUTIFUL, SUNNY DAY in mid-June, and Toi and Keahi were seated on black vinyl chairs at the United Airlines baggage claim area waiting for Liko's plane to arrive. Earlier they had stopped at an airport lei stand, and Toi had picked out a dark-green *ti* lei. It hung from her right forearm and she admired its craftsmanship, nervously.

"I can hardly wait," Toi said. She was dressed simply: black slippers, beige shorts and a T-shirt with a surrealistic picture on the front of a dolphin swimming with children.

She seemed apprehensive to Keahi. But then, he acknowledged to himself that he was apprehensive, too. The last time he had seen Liko was also two years ago, shortly after a young diver had drowned. And now he was visiting Hawaii. Why?

As passengers entered the baggage claim area, Keahi searched the travel-weary faces, wondering what Liko would look like after two years.

Keahi looked for a heavy-set, 20-year-old kid, and consequently, he almost didn't recognize him. *My goodness, he's lost 30 or more pounds!* Keahi was astounded. *He's no longer the overweight kid that I met at the airport several years ago. He's grown an inch, maybe two. He must be six-foot-four to six-foot-five.* The gentle features of his face—the broad, flat nose and large lips that broke quickly into a smile when he saw Toi—had remained the same, though. And those features still reminded Keahi of Liko's father before gambling and alcohol had changed his brother-in-law's countenance.

Keahi watched as Toi stepped forward and held out the open lei. Liko bowed and she slipped it over his large head and onto his broad shoulders. Then they exchanged heartfelt kisses on each other's cheeks, and held each other for a moment in a warm hug. Toi's eyes brimmed with tears as she adjusted the lei around his neck and moved it slightly backwards on his shoulders. Then she stepped back and looked at him.

Her eyes glistened.

Then it was Keahi's turn, and he stepped forward and greeted Liko warmly, kissing him on both cheeks, too. Then they embraced and patted each other several times on the back.

"You're looking great, Liko," Keahi said.

"Thanks, I've been doing a lot of swimming."

Liko, on the other hand, noted that Keahi looked smaller. He turned to Toi, politely looked her up and down, and said: "You are so pretty!"

Keahi saw a warm blush appear in her cheeks.

"How was your flight?" she asked.

"Uneventful. I started a new book, though, *Aquaculture in the Pacific.*"

"Any good?" Keahi asked.

"Not bad. It's about raising fish in coastal waters."

"You must be tired," Toi said.

"Yes, very tired. Flying and driving, they both tire me out!"

"Well, let's get your bags," Keahi said.

As they strolled to the baggage claim, he added. "Remember when your suitcase was stolen?"

Liko laughed—it was the family laugh—and shook his head. "How could I forget? I had packed all my valuables in that suitcase. Yeah, when I came to visit you that first time, Keahi, I didn't intend to return home. My plans were to move in with you and never return to Mom's trailer park."

As their eyes met, Liko realized that Keahi had known about the escape plans all along.

"How is she?" Toi asked.

"My mom? Same as usual, drinking too much." He misstepped and his foot scuffed the buffed floor.

"My sister always was a heavy drinker, even when she was your age," Keahi said.

"I helped her move into an apartment," Liko added. "She's closer to work and has better neighbors."

Liko draped his arm around Toi and gave her another hug—actually, more of a squeeze against the side of his body.

He no longer carries himself like a big kid, Keahi thought. *He's mature: his voice, his manners, his appearance. I wonder what Toi thinks?*

And there was something else. Liko seemed weary, not just travel-weary, but ... weary. Keahi recalled a quote: "A man travels the world over in search of what he needs and returns home to find it." He wondered if that described Liko's experience.

Liko, for his part, sensed that something was different about Keahi. Liko's eyes met Toi's and asked inquiringly what was different. She gave a nod of her head that conveyed the message: "I'll tell you later."

They reached the baggage carousel as the suitcases arrived.

"There're my bags," Liko said, pointing at two large blue bags.

Keahi bent over and grabbed both bags. He grimaced when he lifted them off the carousel. Liko noticed. It was a look of sharp pain.

Liko stepped forward and quickly took both suitcases from Keahi. "I've got them." He popped out the recessed handles and set the suitcases upright on their wheels.

"I'll take this one," Keahi said, reaching for the larger suitcase.

"No, no," Liko said. "If I take both, it keeps me balanced." He rolled the two suitcases behind him, and the small wheels clattered rhythmically on the small, polished floor tiles.

When they reached Keahi's Neon, Liko loaded the larger suitcase in the trunk and the smaller suitcase behind the driver's seat. He then took a seat up front with Keahi. Toi climbed in the back seat, behind Liko. Liko stretched out his long legs and threw his muscular arm across the back of the car seat and behind Keahi's shoulders. Toi leaned forward and rested a hand on Liko's bicep, which bulged almost as large as his head.

As they passed through the downtown area on the H1, Liko turned in his seat towards Toi, and said, point blank, "I wish I could say 'It's great to be back in Hawaii.'" The traffic was bumper-to-bumper as they drove from the airport into Honolulu. "How have things been since the cleanup?"

"They're getting back to normal," Toi said.

"This road is still butt ugly. And the traffic is still the worst in the country."

The Willows restaurant was the perfect setting for a reunion dinner. When Liko had asked Toi to dinner, she had suggested The Willows. She'd commented on the menu: "The buffet is *ono*. It has *kalua* pig, *lomi lomi* salmon, *laulau*, *haupia*, sweet potato and even *poi*."

Now seated at the table across from Toi, next to the replica of the *Hokulea*, a ship named after Arcturus, the zenith star above Hawaii, and with his plate filled with Hawaiian dishes, Liko joked, "Almost as good as fish and chips."

He swallowed a spoonful of the *lomi lomi* salmon, a mixture of salted pink and red salmon, diced tomatoes, chopped green and yellow onions. "Needs a little vinegar."

"Vinegar!"

"Yeah, vinegar. It's the fish-and-chips spice of London. Got used to it there."

Liko finished everything on his plate, then made a second trip through the buffet. After his third trip, Toi asked about his European travels. She started by asking him why he had chosen Europe instead of China, Japan, Hong Kong, and Thailand.

Liko's answer was simple. "My great-aunt was paying the bills, and she insisted that I travel through Italy and Greece first. Once I got there, I just . . . seemed to settle in."

"So what happened?"

Liko hesitated; he didn't want to say anything that would upset her, such as telling her about the girl he had met in Florence. A lot had happened in Venice, too, where he had followed the girl. And then there were the trips to Spain and South America. He had resolved to tell Toi everything, but it had to be at the proper time. So, for now, he told her about a few of the interesting cities that he had visited, like Barcelona and Buenos Aires. After that, he changed the subject.

"Is it my imagination or is Keahi still recovering? When he pulled my suitcase off the conveyor belt he seemed to be in pain."

"He *is* in pain. And he favors his right side, where he was stabbed."

"It still hurts?"

"He lost a kidney, you know. I wrote to you about that, didn't I?"

"Yes, you did."

"It was a savage beating, much worse than any of us realized at the time. The knife damaged not only his kidney but also his liver. And they had to remove one of his ribs, too."

"Damn! Did they find the punk? The one with the hyena pendant?"

"No."

Liko finished his *haupia*—a solid, white square made of coconut milk, sugar, vanilla and cornstarch—and then pushed his plate to the side of the table, clearing the space directly in front of him.

"What are your plans?"

"I'm here to dive the caves," Liko said solemnly, knowing his answer would upset her.

He was right. He watched as the color drained from her face. Her honest, concerned reaction upset him. Nevertheless, he had set the caves as his goal.

"The caves?" she repeated in disbelief.

"I've got a good buddy, so don't worry. She'll be visiting in a few days. And I've trained."

"Have you forgotten that a diver drowned?"

Liko felt as if Toi had reached across the table and slapped him. *No,* he thought.

And I have not forgotten about the girl who drowned in the quarry, either. "I should have warned her about the dive."

"Her?"

Liko realized he had spoken his thought aloud. "I was thinking about someone else, a different dive."

Toi looked at Liko and a worried expression crossed her face.

"I have a lot to tell you." He paused. "There was someone else who drowned before I met you."

Her expression was one of puzzlement. "But the caves," Toi said, "are you really going to attempt the caves?"

"Yes. I am." He looked intently at her. "And not the easy ones at Shark's Cove. We're going to the Big Island."

Her expression was now easy to read. *She thinks I have lost my mind!*

Thank God I didn't tell her about the abduction I prevented in Rome!

Recalling the ambush, he held his breath a moment. He had killed someone.

Liko had no doubt now that his reaction had been a protective reflex. It had been spontaneous.

Nevertheless, it had left him wondering about himself.

What is it like to take a life? It was kind of like the dive in the Nevada quarry that he had survived when he was working towards his diving certification. Yes, it was like that, like crossing a layer of suspended silt. One moment is filled with light. The next moment is pitch black. A Cimmerian blackness. And then one is left struggling to return to the light, to surface, and to breathe again.

How was he going to tell Toi that?

CHAPTER TWENTY-ONE

Kwon sat on Keahi's lanai sipping a glass of water with a squeeze of kumquat as he told Keahi all about it. "Last night I went to see Masako. I brought her a rock—the most beautiful rock that I could find."

"A rock?" Keahi grinned, unable to hide his amusement. "You gave Masako a rock?"

"It's something I learned from Yukio."

Keahi's thoughts went back to the old fisherman. He had built two rock gardens—one at Jack's beach house and the other in the courtyard at work. And then he thought of the old fisherman's great grandson, Ned, who had also helped build both gardens. Lamentably, Ned was still missing. Keahi often wondered what had happened to him.

"Why would you give Masako a rock?" He knew the answer but he wanted to hear Kwon say it.

"It's an old legend. I researched it. Around 600 AD a Chinese emperor presented a rock to a Japanese empress."

"You're kidding me?"

"I guess that sounds strange. But according to the legend, it was an unusually beautiful rock, and the Empress was very pleased."

Keahi raised an eyebrow. He wasn't sure if he should be saddened or amused. He chuckled. "So, did our empress take out a temporary restraining order last night?"

"No, she didn't."

"And why not?"

"Do you want me to tell you about it or not?"

Keahi heard the despondency in Kwon's voice. He also saw the depression of spirit in his face. The loss of hope caught him off guard, surprised him. *I shouldn't have joked about the rock.* He reached across the table and pressed down on Kwon's hand, gently, briefly. "I'm sorry. I'm sure it was a very nice rock."

"Don't patronize me," Kwon quipped, pulling back his hand.

"My bad. I am sorry."

"Her father passed away," Kwon said.

"I know. I saw the obituary."

The extensive obituary had been in the Sunday paper. The paper had run not only a story about Mr. Hasahimoto, but also his photo. The eulogy had listed numerous charitable projects that Mr. Hasahimoto had funded, had praised his liberal contributions to the arts, and had commended him for his work in the community, including his long tenure on the State Land Use Commission. According to the paper, the funeral would be local style: lei only, aloha attire, cremation to follow.

Keahi added, "And I went to the funeral."

"So did I."

Since Kwon and Masako didn't get along, and since Kwon had never said anything good about Masako's father, why would he attend the funeral? "I don't remember seeing you there."

"I was in the back. I saw you."

Keahi recalled his conversation with Masako as they stood together, briefly, beside her father's coffin. She had shared that she had found her father in his study, sitting in his leather chair, behind his koa desk, with a frown on his face, his eyes wide open, his hands clutching his chest. That's how she had described it. His eyes wide open!

Keahi considered sharing all those details with Kwon. But instead, he only looked at him and shook his head.

"Poor Masako," Kwon said. "First her brother and now her father."

Keahi took a deep breath. "Tell me about your rock."

"Last night I visited her and I gave her the rock. I told her that I was sorry about her loss. I asked her if there was anything, anything at all, that I could do for her."

Keahi nodded.

"I'm very worried about her," Kwon volunteered.

Keahi placed his hand gently on Kwon's shoulder.

Each withdrew into their own thoughts and there was a long, melancholy lull in their conversation.

Not knowing what to say, Keahi ventured a new subject: "Liko is back."

"For the summer?"

"Maybe, at least long enough to dive some caves."

"No!" Kwon shook his head. "After so many drowned?"

"I'm afraid so."

"Is he staying with you?"

"Not this time. He's staying with my aunt." Keahi added, "Toi wants me to stop him."

"Can you do that?"

"I don't know how."

"Why cave diving?"

"Why give Masako a rock?"

They sat together, both dejected.

CHAPTER TWENTY-TWO

Liko hovered above the labyrinth's portal, demonstrating good buoyancy control before he dropped into the 10 foot diameter hole and descended 30 feet to the sandy ocean floor. Hovering, he surveyed the sides of the portal until he found a lava tube entrance.

The ocean surge buffeted him. He watched the water swirl and stir up the sand beneath him, creating a sand funnel. The entrance to the side tube, a prehistoric underwater tube like the above-ground Thurston Lava tube, clouded.

Liko had heard that the side tube sloped gradually along its three-kilometer length to a depth of 110 feet, before reopening to the ocean. And he had been warned that this particular formation sported shark tooth lavacicles that allowed a diver to pass in one direction only, like a fish trap. Of course, he hadn't told Toi about the three-kilometer length or the 110-foot depth or the lavacicles.

Liko checked his flashlights; both were working fine. He checked his dive partner; his friend Lori was by his side, attached by a line. A native of England, they had met earlier in the year in London, where she was taking a break from her passion: documenting natural labyrinths, above- and below-ground, dry and underwater. It was like a religion, or more accurately, it was like a religious experience for her. In fact, Lori was so enthusiastic about lava tubes that she had spent the previous year as a National Park Service guide in the Lava Beds National Monument, exploring the dry underground tubes. She was a self-described lava tube junky. She was also a successful artist whose depictions of labyrinths, both man-made and natural, had won her international attention. She was even published, with a coffee table book highlighting her best pottery designs and sand paintings, many based on natural labyrinths that she had explored.

Now, hovering with Lori, Liko calculated their risk and felt confident. Before him stretched a challenge, guaranteed to heighten his awareness, and he craved that.

Lori signaled him and entered the tube. He followed, attached by a line. A tidal surge filled the entrance behind them with silt. Liko shone a beam at the boiling sand. It was like a door, closing.

He focused ahead on the tube. He felt a strong pulsing current, as if the walls themselves were contracting. Calmly and deliberately, they negotiated their way.

They descended along a gradual slope until their dive consoles read 50 feet. After that, they carefully weaved through wall after wall of shark tooth lavacicles, soon passing multiple points of no return. And then there was a gradual narrowing of the tube, until they had to slip out of their jackets and tanks to pass through a choke point, an occlusion in the channel like plaque in an artery. They held their jackets and tanks in front of them as they slipped through body-sized occlusions.

The younger, fatter Liko would not have fit; the new Liko, just barely. The rush of water passing through the choke points reminded him of the narrow cable passage through the inner reef at Hanauma Bay. He recalled how the Venturi effect had sucked him past razor-sharp coral. Now, in the lava tube, a gentle current continually pushed from behind.

When they came to a Y in the tunnel, they checked their dive consoles to verify the depth. It was 110 feet deep. Local divers had advised Lori that the tunnel to the left was a dead-end. Divers had taken it and drowned. So Lori ventured to the right and Liko followed.

After 20 yards, daylight gradually appeared. They began a slow ascent. As the sun grew brighter and brighter Liko could barely contain a feeling of ecstasy. *This is where I belong, in the ocean, in all the fullness of life.*

On the surface, while Lori congratulated him, he silently cried, the tears mixing with salt water and disappearing into the ocean.

I must be narked!

After that, they swam ashore.

Toi was waiting for him. She watched, relieved and proud, as he made a graceful shore exit. Lori, however, fell, which greatly amused a group of tourists.

Liko loaded his gear into his new pewter-colored Nissan truck, which he had purchased earlier in the week. Lori had a sporty rental car. After that, he and Lori shook hands and said goodbye.

Liko then found himself alone with Toi.

"We almost cancelled today."

"Why?"

He grinned. "The water was cloudy."

She balled up her small hand and punched him on his massive shoulder.

She loves me, he thought.

He shrugged his shoulder and the muscles stood out, well-defined. "I want to be a Master Dive Instructor."

She gave him a hug, said she was happy for him.

Then he said that he had applied to Hawaii Pacific University. He told her that he was starting classes in the fall in the marine biology and oceanography program. He said he was interested in studying deep reefs and the deep sea floor, where sunlight is absent, but where monk seals and humpback whales swim, and golden coral grows.

"Where are you going to room?" she asked.

"That's a problem," he said. He already knew about the severe shortage of campus housing. In fact, he had been counseled that most students left campus immediately after their classes ended for the day and lived off-campus. "I dunno, but I can't stay at my aunt's forever, can I?"

"How about my place?" Toi offered.

"I'd like that," Liko answered. "I'd like that a lot."

He wrapped an arm around her and the two of them sat on the tailgate of his new Nissan truck, looking out over the ocean. The ocean looked calm and peaceful.

Toi rested her head on his shoulder.

CHAPTER TWENTY-THREE

"Hello," Santos answered his work phone.

"This is Aloha Pics. We have an unclaimed photo—an eight-and-a-half by eleven dropped off by Larry Williams. Is someone going to pick it up? We've had it a long time."

Santos's heart skipped a beat. "I'll be right there."

"It's seven dollars: two dollars for scanning the photo and five dollars for the CD."

"I'll be there in five minutes."

He hurriedly signed out on the board in the clerical area and left for the photo store. Twenty minutes later, he was sitting in his big Buick, parked in two spaces next to a massive, green, concrete pillar in the lowest level of the Ala Moana Shopping Mall. He held a large, glossy photo in his chubby hands. He gazed at it: a swing set in a playground.

A look of relief came into his pudgy face. *The Captain will be pleased! Very pleased!*

He looked closely at the photo, studied it. In the background, behind the swing set and up a slight incline, was the parking lot of the former laundry facility, now Club Kesago. His eyes scanned the black surface of the parking lot. He saw nothing unusual. He scanned the back wall of the club. He saw a pipe running up the back of the building. It was a vent line. A vent line from an underground storage tank! Surprised, he breathed in sharply. It was evidence of a second tank!

He noticed, also, that the oleander hedge was missing. No, not missing, just severely trimmed back. He tried to recall the height of the hedge. Was it eight feet tall? He couldn't remember. But it was tall. Yes, it was tall and thick. *In fact*, he thought, *if someone stood in the playground today, the hedge would block their view.* Yes, it would block their view. They would see neither the parking lot nor the club. He smiled, proud that he had the picture.

He wondered if the vent line had been removed. Yes, surely the Captain—or Alegado—had removed the vent line from the exterior wall, just like they had gotten rid of the tank, during the night, secretly. But had they?

Santos thought: *If they removed the vent line then all evidence of a second tank is gone—except for this photo.*

He asked aloud: "What should I do?"

Hooonk!

Santos jumped in his car seat. He looked in the rearview mirror of his big Buick and saw a woman driver, urging him to pull out of his two parking spaces.

How rude! He wasn't ready to leave! Annoyed, he waved her on.

She gave him the stink eye and shouted, "Learn to park, jerk," and squealed off.

He countered by giving her the finger, but low enough behind the car door so she couldn't see it.

Then he refocused on the photo, continuing to study it: there was something else, he could sense it.

He stared at the photo a long time, studied the building, the parking lot, the cars in the parking lot, the license plates. One seemed familiar . . .

Yes! The Captain's big body Benz!

"Good God!" Santos said out loud as he discovered the full importance of the picture. He held the picture close to his good right eye and squinted. He could clearly see the registration sticker on the tag. *This picture isn't that old! It certainly is not as old as the child care center administrator thinks. Oleander must be a fast growing hedge. This picture is only two, maybe three years old.*

Suddenly a thought popped into his mind: *Did Little Bill figure all this out, too?*

Then another thought: *Did he contact the Captain?*

And then a terrible thought: *If so, did the Captain have something to do with the explosion at the meth lab? Or was that a coincidence?*

Santos shook his head in disbelief, vehemently denying that possibility, even though he was holding the evidence in his hands.

"I had nothing to do with Little Bill's death!" He said this out loud in the privacy of his big Buick. But he felt no absolution. Instead he felt numb.

He slid the photo back into the envelope and set it on the passenger seat. Then he started up his big Buick, pulled out of the parking spaces, and drove back to the office as if on autopilot, unaware of anything, as if his brain had shut down.

Eventually the numbness would wear off, like a tingling shot of Novocain. The disorientation that followed the numbness was so intense that it would remain with Santos for weeks afterward.

That afternoon, before Santos decided what to do with the photo and the CD, Jack called a staff meeting. Santos didn't want to attend, but he also didn't want to call attention to himself, so he dragged himself to the meeting, reluctantly. Arriving late, he surveyed the room and saw Jack and his 'team' seated around the table. The rest of the staff were seated along the surrounding walls. He saw that only one chair remained. It was at the table and directly across from Jack. Santos reluctantly sat down, placing his black day planner and loose papers in his lap, holding them as if protecting them from his coworkers.

Jack began by thanking everyone for coming. Then he explained how recent election results would affect the department: the new governor already had appointed a new director general. And Jack was losing his job, too, effective the first of next month. The constant complaints being made by Santos, with the support of the union, obviously had not helped Jack's standing with the incoming administration.

After thanking everyone for their support, Jack said, "I am dissolving the team, effective immediately."

Everyone was stunned except for Santos, who was pleased. *Good riddance to both of them—Jack and the team.* It was his opinion that the team was little more than an extension of Jack's ego, anyway.

He ran his finger over the edge of his day planner. A brown envelope containing the photo of the swing set was tucked inside. He had decided that the photo was too valuable to leave in his office, unattended, so he had brought it with him to the meeting.

Now, hearing Jack announce that he would soon be dismissed, Santos's mind began to relax. *As soon as he is gone, I'm going to discipline Keahi.* With that thought he began to feel a bit better. *Maybe I can even find an excuse to fire him.* He scooted his chair back, scuffing the floor.

Jack cleared his throat, this time to get everyone's attention. "Before I adjourn our last meeting, does anyone have anything they would like to say?"

Not me, Santos thought, settling back in his seat. *I can finally relax!*

"Yes," Masako spoke up. "I have something that I'd like to say."

For God's sake, Santos thought, *keep it short.* He closed his eyes and allowed his mind to wander. Soon he began to daydream.

In his daydream, Masako said, "As most of you already know, my father passed away earlier this year." Several of the members had not heard, and Masako waited as they expressed their condolences, then she thanked them for their sympathy.

She continued: "My father's estate is now officially settled, and I will inherit everything."

Lucky bitch, Santos thought, daydreaming. *She gets his money, his marriage business, even his house on Tantalus.*

"I now have everything, including a key to his safe deposit box at the Bank of Hawaii, that in turn contained the combination to his safe."

Now that's interesting, Santos thought, still daydreaming.

"And in his safe I found a yellow notebook." She paused, choosing her words carefully. "The notebook describes unrecorded *huis* that he belonged to when he was serving on the State Land Use Commission."

Why is she looking at me so pointedly, Santos wondered.

Her piercing eyes jarred something in his distant memory, and he asked himself, *Why would she tell us about her father's huis?*

"I brought his notebook with me this morning. If Kwon will accept it, I would like to give it to him."

Santos glanced from Misako to Kwon. Kwon appeared flabbergasted. Stunned, he graciously accepted.

"I think it will be of interest to all of you, especially the history of one particular *hui* – a small group of investors who profited from the decisions my father made while he was on the State Land Use Commission. This notebook contains the names of some of our most respected community leaders."

Santos followed Masako's gaze as she looked around the table at everyone. She saw tears of joy on Kwon's face. Her eyes met Kwon's and she nodded, bowed slightly, and smiled respectfully. *Unbelievable*, Santos thought. *This must be a dream!*

"The members of this *hui* profited when my father voted to rezone agricultural lands to industrial use, and when he voted to rezone rural lands to residential use. The members of this *hui*—including my father—made a lot of money."

Jesus! Santos thought. *What's the matter with her? She's ruining her father's name, her family's reputation, her father's business—all of which now belong to her.*

"Who are the members?" Lim asked.

"Politicians. Good ol' boys. You will recognize their names. Some have passed on."

"So what does this have to do with us?" Lim asked.

"Everything, Lim," Masako said. "Everything."

Masako paused for a moment, carefully choosing her words. She looked directly at Kwon, speaking slow and clear. "Kwon, I think you should compare the members of this particular *hui* to the property owners who used the 'Black Box Lab.'"

Santos gripped his day planner tightly, pressed it against his lap. He looked down and saw that his knuckles had turned white against the black leather.

"Sure," Kwon said, smiling broadly. "I'll compare them, right away."

"I predict that you will find a strong correlation between the two lists," Masako said.

"And I bet all of the properties are grossly contaminated," Lim stated.

"I wouldn't be surprised," Masako said.

"Santos," she continued, her head now cocked to one side, "do you have anything that you want to tell us?"

For a moment, the room became deadly silent. Santos could hear himself wheezing.

"Why?" Santos said, breaking the silence. "Why?"

"Because your name is in this notebook, Santos," Masako said. "How in the world did *your* name get in this notebook?"

Kwon, seated to the left of Santos, reached for Santos's day planner in anger, yanking it out of his hands. "Answer her, Santos," Kwon demanded, now waving his hands in Santos's face. "Answer her."

Santos's heart was pounding in his chest.

Kwon slammed his fists down on the table.

The planner seemed to leap from Santos's lap. He tried to control it but it suddenly exploded as if detonated.

Keahi thought that Santos had either just had a stroke or was having a heart attack. His hands jerked spastically and the contents of his planner flew in all directions. Several papers, including a brown envelope, sailed underneath the table and came to rest beneath Jack's chair.

"Are you okay?" Keahi asked Santos. He placed his hand on Santos's arm and shook him gently.

"What!" Santos exclaimed, slamming out of his daydream.

Santos was surprised to suddenly find himself in a meeting with his coworkers. He was deeply confused for a few seconds, but then he regained his bearings and shrugged off Keahi's hand. He noticed that Masako was now seated, but he couldn't recall what she had said.

"I just..." he mumbled.

"Are you okay?" Keahi asked again.

"You're all a bunch of idiots," Santos mumbled, looking at Keahi, again pulling away from him.

Keahi raised an eyebrow, shocked by such an untimely, inappropriate comment. Nevertheless, Keahi helped him pick up the planner and a CD. He placed them into Santos's trembling hands.

Santos instinctively closed his fingers, grasping the planner and CD jewel case. He mindlessly slipped the case into the planner. He then abruptly pushed his chair away from the table, stood up, and left the room.

The brown envelope remained underneath Jack's chair, unnoticed.

Santos dropped his day planner on his desk and went directly to the restroom. When he returned to his office he found Keahi waiting for him, looking at pictures of his family—Filipina and his daughters—on his desk. Santos's planner was open, too.

"What are you doing?"

"I'm giving notice," Keahi said, shifting his weight from one foot to the other, uneasily. "I quit."

Santo stared at him in disbelief. *That's not possible.* He looked at the open planner on his desk. *He is just saying that to draw attention away from the fact that he just took the photo. He's not going to quit. He's not stupid.*

His eyes focused on Keahi. Where did he hide it? Was it under his shirt? Was it in his work papers that he was holding at his side?

Keahi saw the distraught expression on Santo's face. *He disapproves of my decision to quit. Or maybe he doesn't believe me.*

Santos smiled and said, "If you want to play games that's fine with me."

Puzzled, Keahi stared at him. Santos was smiling. How strange. He waited for Santos to explain what he meant by 'play games,' but he didn't. Instead, he just stood in front of him, silent and smiling.

Confused, Keahi shook his head, turned and walked out of the office.

Santos sat down in his chair behind his desk. He ruffled through his planner.

The loss of the photograph was bad news. He sighed. The Captain was not going to be happy.

CHAPTER TWENTY-FOUR

SEATED IN THE NIGHTCLUB, Santos told the Captain everything: how he had returned from the restroom and found Keahi in his office; how Keahi had been looking at the pictures on his desk; how Keahi had suddenly given him notice that he was resigning. But most important, Santos told the Captain that Keahi had stolen the photo of the playground equipment. Yes, it had been stolen. Santos had picked it up at the photo shop, he had put it in his planner, but then Keahi had stolen it right off his desk, right out of his planner! Fortunately, he still had the compact disc with the digital image, but the photo was gone.

"As soon as you had it, you should have brought it to me," the Captain said, his voice rising. "Why did you wait?"

"I was in the restroom. He came into my office while I was in the restroom. He took it out of my planner. How was I supposed to know he'd do that?"

The Captain paced back and forth in front of the black door at the back of his club, frowning at everyone in the dimly lit room. Santos saw Alegado and even the body-guard cringe.

"That faggot's caused me enough trouble!" The Captain's voice quivered with anger. "First the tank. Then the plume. Now the photo. His interference must stop!"

"I'll take care of it," the bodyguard volunteered.

"Damn right you will!" the Captain yelled, his body trembling with rage.

Then he turned and gave Santos a sharp, disapproving look. His eyes were blazing. "Some people you can depend on, others you can't."

Santos felt like the Captain had drawn a bow and shot him through with an arrow.

Later in the week, Santos was walking around outside his office building. He had indigestion from eating too large a lunch, and he was hoping fresh air would help. Instead, the exertion had robbed him of his breath and had left him huffing and puffing. He was sweating profusely. Now, as he came around the corner of the building and approached the front door, he was anxious to get back into the air conditioning.

That's when he overheard two employees gossiping by the front door. "The caller told him to put his affairs in order—" One of the employees made a cutting motion with his hand across his throat.

"Any idea who it was?" the other asked.

"No, no idea at all. But it has to be a nut."

They shifted their feet and moved aside as Santos walked by and entered the building. He wanted to stop and listen, but he continued walking; he didn't want to draw attention to himself. He wondered if they were talking about Keahi and the death threat.

Santos knew that Keahi had followed the proper procedures: he had reported the death threat to him—because he was his supervisor—and then Keahi had reported it to the police. But the police were unable to help. Keahi had so little information to tell them: a man with a voice like gravel said 'Put your affairs in order.' What could the police do with that?

Last time they almost killed him, Santos thought, out of breath and miserable. He imagined the Captain's bodyguard, the big Samoan, pouncing on Keahi, striking a blow to his head, destroying his remaining kidney.

Santos now knew that the bodyguard was pathologically sadistic. Why else would he call up Keahi and give him such a hellish message? It was just like when he threw the life preserver to the girl, knowing that she was going to be devoured by sharks. Why would someone do that? It was worse than a cat playing with a mouse. Santos wondered if the bodyguard was even human. How could a human behave like that? And Santos was also sure that the Captain didn't know that the bodyguard was toying with Keahi. That wasn't the way the Captain did business. The Captain didn't like complications. But hell, Santos thought. I'm not going to tell him. Why would I invite the wrath of the bodyguard directed at me? I'm not crazy.

He shook his head. Keahi had no chance, no chance at all. He was as good as dead.

There's nothing I can do. He was breathing heavily, was out of breath, was dizzy. His chubby face was red. *No, it's too late.*

Late Friday evening, Keahi finished a half-hearted workout and strolled down Kalakaua Avenue through Waikiki. When he came to Gandhi's statue he stopped to admire it. He leaned against the pedestal, facing the statue, the ocean, and the setting sun.

"What's going on, babu?"

Gandhi did not reply.

"Did I make the right choice, babu?"

He imagined Gandhi's reply: "I am proud of you, Keahi. It takes great courage to start a new life."

Kwon heard about the threat firsthand from Keahi. He then told Toi, and she, in turn, told Liko.

"Who threatened you?" Liko demanded, talking to Keahi on his cell phone.

"I don't know. It was just a voice on the phone. An irritated, damaged voice."

"Who has a beef with you?"

"I have no idea."

"Was it a crank call?"

"No, he was serious."

"How do you know?"

"The severity of his voice. The way he told me to 'get my affairs in order.'"

A cold shudder moved up and down Liko's spine, and his body jerked once, involuntarily. "Be careful!"

The tone of Liko's voice left Keahi feeling even more nervous.

CHAPTER TWENTY-FIVE

THE ROCK CLASSIC *YES, I AM* WAS PLAYING as Angelica finished setting the dinner table; the raw emotion of Melissa Etheridge's raspy voice filled the small condominium. Keahi relaxed in a comfortable chair. Carol folded her legs beneath her on the loveseat. Together, the three of them were listening to the triple platinum album.

"Do you need anything?" Angelica asked.

"Some wine, please," Carol said.

"Same here," Keahi chimed in.

A back issue of *Rolling Stone Magazine* lay open on the table. Keahi picked it up. It was an old issue, January 2000. The magazine's pages were dog-eared.

Angelica served them each a glass of Burgundy, then sat down next to Carol on the loveseat.

The two women leaned against each other, held hands and smiled. Keahi thought that their smiles were rather tense. And he thought that their eyes glowed with mischief: Angelica's a bright green and Carol's a deep chocolate brown.

Something is up, he thought, *and it undoubtedly has something to do with me.*

"Set your glass down," Carol ordered.

"What?"

"Please, set your wine glass down on the coffee table."

Keahi shot her a quizzical look.

"I don't want you to spill it," Carol explained. "I have something to say, and I don't want you to spill red wine all over our white carpet, okay?"

"Sure," Keahi agreed, "no problem."

He set his almost full wine glass down on the edge of the coffee table.

Sitting side-by-side, holding hands, Carol and Angelica stared at him.

"What?" Keahi asked, growing concerned. "What did I do?"

Waiting for an answer, he broke eye contact and bowed his head. He stared at the cover of the old *Rolling Stone* issue without consciously seeing the cover. He exhaled, nervously. He felt the room vibrating with the electric blues rock.

Finally, Carol began: "There is a special bonding between a birth mother and her child."

"Yeah?" Keahi said, raising his eyes to Carol.

"And we want to experience it," Angelica said.

"Oh," Keahi said, glancing over at Angelica. He shrugged. He didn't see what *that* had to do with him.

"And we want our children to be related by blood," Carol added.

"I see," Keahi said, although he didn't.

"And we want you to be the uncle!" Angelica said, blurting it out.

"But without parental responsibilities," Carol quickly added.

"I see," Keahi said again, but he still had no idea what they were talking about.

"Carol and I would be the parents."

"Parents?"

"Yes, for each other's child."

"Oh," Keahi said.

"So, what do you think?" Carol asked Keahi.

"About what?"

"Being the father of our children," Angelica said.

He bolted upright and the side of his leg bumped the coffee table and the glass full of wine spilled.

They looked down at the wine glass now resting on the white carpet surrounded by a bright red pattern. Nothing more needed to be said. They realized that their relationship had just undergone a sudden and irreversible change.

CHAPTER TWENTY-SIX

MORE THAN FIFTY PEOPLE ATTENDED, including Liko, yet the baby's first birthday was still considered a small turnout by local standards. Keahi had once attended a party of a hundred kids, not including the parents.

With Kwon, he hunted down the birthday kid—which was easy because Limen was holding him.

Keahi spotted them first. He wanted to get a good look at the kid. "I wonder how much he's grown?"

"During the first four years of life, the human brain triples in size," Kwon said as they walked across the room to join Limen, Lim, and their baby boy.

"No!"

"It's a fact," Kwon said.

"Lim, Limen, how are you guys?" Keahi raised his voice as they approached.

"Not bad," Lim and Limen replied, almost in unison.

"And the little one?" Keahi asked.

"This little guy?" Lim paused briefly as he took his son from Limen. "He'll be walking soon."

"No!" Keahi repeated.

"Oh yeah!" Lim said. "Let me show you." He gently set his son on the floor in a seated position. Then he reached down, and when the baby gripped his index fingers, he pulled him upright. Lim shuffled backwards, slowly, guiding his son, encouraging him to walk. The baby slapped the ground with his feet, holding tightly onto Lim's fingers for balance. He had a big baby smile.

Lim pulled his fingers away, suddenly. The baby looked at his father in amazement, as his small arms flailed at his side. He found himself standing alone, on his own two feet. He picked up his right foot and slapped it down flat on the floor—he hadn't learned to put his heel down first—and he tumbled sideways. His feet went into the air and his head into the floor, which he hit hard. He began to cry.

Lim's face filled with disappointment. "Soon. He will walk soon," he said, his voice serious.

Limen scooped up the wailing baby into her arms.

"Amazing!" Keahi said. "He is so confident! So fearless!"

Keahi wondered what it would be like to coach a son to walk, to swim, to lift weights. To be there for him when he fell? To encourage him to try again?

"I'll do it," he said.

"Do what?" Limen asked.

"Oh, sorry," Keahi said. "I was thinking out loud."

I'll be the father of their children. And I'll have two sons, not one.

"Why don't we all go to the zoo next weekend?" he suggested. "Let's get the old team together for another outing. What do you think?"

Lim, Limen and Kwon didn't look enthusiastic about his idea.

"It's a fun place for *keiki*," he added.

"Have you received any more death threats?" Lim asked.

"Just that one," Keahi replied, taken aback that Lim would bring up that subject at his son's birthday party. "It's past. As you know, I don't work at the department anymore."

Liko, standing nearby, surrounded by a group of parents and their kids, overheard the question and Keahi's reply. He bit his tongue, stopping himself from following up on Keahi's answer. He wanted to know what Keahi's colleagues knew about the threat.

"Keahi won't tell me anything," Liko complained to Kwon, later, when he caught Kwon alone.

"That's because he doesn't know anything."

"Well, who does?" Liko asked. He found the situation frustrating, intolerable.

Kwon shook his head.

"Could the threat be connected to the lab that burned down?"

"I don't see how," Kwon answered. "We're no longer working that case."

"Why not?"

"It's now part of an arson investigation. We don't investigate arsons."

"Well, what about the playground explosion?"

"No, I doubt that that has anything to do with it, either."

"Why?"

"You don't know?" Kwon asked.

"Know what?"

"Keahi was taken off that case a long time ago, before the oil spill happened. Santos is working it now."

Liko's brow furrowed. He didn't know.

"So, no one involved with the arson or the explosion would have any reason to be angry at him?"

"Not that I can think of."

"Then who is threatening him?"

"I have no idea."

"Does it have something to do with the gang that attacked him?"

"I don't know."

"Keahi is your friend, isn't he?"

"Of course."

"So why aren't you helping him?"

Liko saw frustration fill Kwon's face, and clearly he was not happy with that last question.

"Listen," he replied sharply, "what am I supposed to do? I don't have any more information than you do."

Liko raised an eyebrow and said, "Why not?"

They stared at each other, and Liko saw anger building in Kwon's face.

"We are all responsible for each other, Kwon." *I learned that the hard way*, Liko said to himself. "So what can we do?"

Kwon shrugged, but Liko saw the expression on Kwon's face change from frustration and anger to determination. *Keahi has a friend*, he thought.

As the party wound down, the team members gathered around the baby and Lim and Limen and said goodbye.

Liko joined them.

"I had hoped Jack would show up," Liko said, disappointment in his voice.

"He has taken the loss of Little Ned badly," Lim said.

"I saw Jack at the Floating Lantern Festival, last month," Masako said. "We floated a lantern for Yukio."

Kwon pursed his lips and nodded.

"He misses Little Ned terribly," Keahi added.

"I would go mad if someone took our son."

"Don't even think such a terrible thing!" Limen interjected.

Liko listened carefully to what everyone said.

Soon Liko was fuming inside. *If someone hurt Keahi I'd bundle 'em up. Yes, I'd bundle 'em.* He had read about it in that magazine during his flight from the Big Island back to Oahu, after the lava tube dive. It was called bundling up: first you overpower your enemy, then you dislocate their joints, then you break every major bone in their bodies, and last, you snap their backs like toothpicks.

Yeah, that's what I'd do . . .

CHAPTER
TWENTY-SEVEN

THAT WEEKEND, KEAHI had a candlelight dinner with Angelica and Carol. They were thrilled that he had agreed to father their children, but there was a problem.

"How are we going to do it?" he asked.

"Sperm bank," Angelica replied quickly.

"You provide the sperm," Carol added, "and we do the rest."

"What a relief!" he said with a heavy sigh and a smile.

"Oh, Keahi," Angelica said. "You didn't think we would—"

"I never know what you ladies are thinking."

"You understand that you will have no legal rights?" Carol asked, emphatically.

"Why not?"

"Because you will have no child custody entitlement."

"What? Why?"

"It's going to be hard enough for Angelica and me," Carol explained.

Angelica added a comment: "Neither of us will have custody rights, either, until we legally adopt each other's baby."

"I see," Keahi said, smiling halfheartedly. "So how do you legally adopt?"

"First we see a family law attorney," Carol replied.

"But I want to be involved in their lives, too," Keahi said, firmly.

"We are only talking about who will *legally* be the parents," Carol said. "We are not talking about whether or not you can see the kids. Of course you can see the kids."

"The custody agreement should include me," he stated, matter-of-factly.

Angelica opened her mouth and started to reply but Carol held her back.

Keahi saw them squeeze hands, hard.

"We'll think about it," Carol said.

The next evening, Angelica and Carol dropped by to see Keahi.

"We agree," Carol began, as they entered the studio. "We'll all share custody of the kids."

"That's great!" Keahi ushered them inside. Suddenly he was a happy man.

They sat down on his large green hide-a-bed couch as he dashed into the kitchen. In a flash, he returned with a bottle of Martini & Rossi Asti. He removed the foil and wire hood and popped the cork. It ricocheted off the concrete ceiling and they all yelled "look out!" in unison. Then he poured three glasses.

Together they watched the bubbles.

"I propose a toast," he said, holding up his glass: "May our children grow up in a caring, loving family with three loving parents!"

They tapped glasses.

"What this means, of course," Carol said, "is that Angelica and I will not adopt each other's baby. You understand that don't you, Keahi? If we adopted each other's baby that would eliminate your rights as the father, essentially severing your rights." She looked at Keahi to make sure that he understood. "You see, a baby can have no more than two legal parents—gay or straight. Period. That's the law. *Three* legal parents is not allowed!"

"Well, that's just another law that needs to be changed," Keahi said, curtly. "After all, three strands are stronger than two, right?"

They then drank the wine and imagined raising two children, simultaneously.

"Like raising fraternal twins," Keahi predicted.

They were giddy with excitement, expectation and hope.

Eventually, they talked about where the babies would live, and they agreed that Angelica and Carol's condominium was too small. Another bedroom was needed. Keahi wished that he had money saved up, something he could give them for a down payment on a small house, but the cost of living was just too high in Hawaii, and, like most locals, he had no savings. And besides, he had just quit his job.

Soon the wine was gone.

Keahi watched as Angelica collected the wine glasses. Then she disappeared into the kitchen, where she washed two of them, thoroughly, in hot, soapy water. And then she returned and handed the two wine glasses to Keahi.

"You'll need these, tonight."

"Why's that?"

"We don't want to use a sperm bank," Carol said.

"I see," Keahi said. But, as usual, he had no idea what they were telling him.

So he watched, bewildered, as Carol rummaged through her large handbag until she found a plastic bag, labeled Longs Drug Store. Then she removed two oral medicine syringes from the bag and set them in the middle of the table.

"What is that?" he asked.

"Something like a turkey baster but without the bulb," she said, smiling.

"For making babies," Angelica added.

"Oh!" Keahi said, blushing. He now understood.

"So the wine glasses . . ."

"Yes," Angelica said.

"I don't think that will work," Keahi said, looking at the supplies now spread out on his table. There was a bottle of saline solution, some tubing, and a small bottle of anti-bacterial soap.

"Maybe," Angelica said, "maybe not."

"But let's try it," Carol said. "If it doesn't work then we can use a sperm bank."

Keahi stared at the two wine glasses. After a few moments he looked at Carol and Angelica. They nodded, grinning at him, their smiles teasing him. He nodded in agreement.

Then Carol reached into her handbag again and pulled out a package wrapped in gold gift wrap with blue and pink ribbons.

"For me?" Keahi asked.

She nodded.

He opened it. It was a small bottle of peppermint scented body lotion.

"I see," he said. And he did, indeed, understand.

Keahi set the two wine glasses on the edge of the bathroom sink. He smiled amiably; it was time to masturbate not once, but twice. *Angelica and Carol know what they're doing*, he thought. And for his part, he knew that he had at least two full ejaculations within him. Last night he had masturbated, which, fortuitously, would have removed any old sperm.

Now he opened the peppermint lotion. He sniffed it.

He emerged from the bathroom with two wine glasses, each covered with a warm washcloth, each containing seed for a future child.

He handed one wine glass to Carol, the other to Angelica.

Their eyes met. He loved Angelica's green eyes with their flecks of gold. And Carol's brown eyes had gone misty, the color of chocolate truffles, twice licked.

"I'll be in the pool," he added. He had changed into his swimsuit. He let himself out of his studio.

The ladies clinked the two wine glasses together and smiled broadly.

The water temperature was perfect. He swam until he was tired. Then he surface-dived repeatedly, until he was out of breath. He pulled himself from the pool and sat on the edge, his feet dangling into the warm water, making small circles that rippled across the surface. He was excited. He felt hyperactive. So he slipped back into the water. He knew he was tired but he had to continue: one more lap. Then another and another and another, until finally, he thrashed his way down the length of the pool, towards the shallow end, utterly exhausted, his body spinning out of control.

His knees found the bottom. He sat upright in the warm water, spent, his head just above water, looking up at his lanai. He was so tired! He was also expectant and hopeful.

His dear friends were now standing on his lanai, holding hands. He waved at them and they waved for him to rejoin them and he knew his sperm was on its way, seeking their eggs.

He went upstairs.

The wine glasses had been washed and set at the back of the kitchen counter, to the right of his kitchen sink.

Keahi and Angelica and Carol hugged.

Then they lay down together on Keahi's large koa wood bed. The three of them talked for a while and then sleep took them.

CHAPTER TWENTY-EIGHT

It was hard to tell who was more surprised, Masako or Keahi. She knocked, and when Keahi opened his apartment door she found the women in his bed. It was an awkward moment until they both smiled and hugged.

Masako's knocking also awakened Angelica and Carol.

Carol sat up and scooted to the edge of the bed, her feet dangling above the floor, her black hair mussed and wild. Sleep still governed her brown eyes, and she yawned. She was wearing white panty briefs and one of Keahi's T-shirts.

Angelica stumbled sleepily from the bed to the bathroom, and said "Good morning" to Masako as she passed her in the short hallway. She closed the bathroom door and Keahi and Masako heard her put the toilet seat down.

"I'll come back later," Masako suggested.

"No, no," Keahi pleaded. "Please come in."

When she still hesitated, he smiled again, and added, shrugging his shoulders, "We're all awake now anyway."

He ushered her into the large studio room and insisted that she sit on the large green sleeper-sofa, which hadn't been used.

They heard Angelica pee.

"So what brings you here so early on a Sunday morning?"

She opened her mouth, but no words came out. She tried to remember why she had dropped by. Then she suddenly remembered and said, "Oh, yes . . . I've decided to manage my father's business. I'm quitting the bureaucracy, too."

Keahi rubbed the palms of his hands across his face, clearing himself of the last of the foggy sleep. What did it mean that she was going to manage her father's business? "What about your work at the department?"

"I've given notice—just like you did, two weeks."

"Whoa!"

They heard the toilet flush and then running water.

"I'm very happy for you," he added, smiling.

Masako's eyes surveyed his apartment and took in Carol, who was still sitting on the edge of his bed, half asleep. "I guess I should be happy for *you*, too."

Now Keahi blushed.

"I need a coordinator," Masako said. "That's why I'm here."

"A coordinator?"

"Yes, a wedding coordinator."

"But I don't know anything about—"

But before Keahi could protest that he knew nothing about weddings, much less how to organize and coordinate them, she interjected, "I need someone I can trust. Someone I can work with. And you can sing and dance and give the weddings a special Hawaiian character. You would be perfect for the job. Besides," she smiled at him, "I know you are unemployed."

That made him smile, too. "I'll think about it."

"We can be your first wedding," Carol suggested from the edge of the bed, awakening. "What do you think? Would you marry us?"

"Sure!" Masako said, sincerely, without any hesitation. "But just you and Angelica, right? I don't do threesomes!"

Keahi's chuckling bounced off the concrete walls.

Angelica opened the bathroom door and joined them, taking a seat next to Masako. She was wearing light green underpants and matching bra. Her green eyes were still sleepy. The emerald in her ear sparkled.

"What's so funny?" she asked, stifling a yawn.

"We're going to a wedding," Carol replied.

"Whose?"

"Ours."

"But I'm not dressed for a wedding," Angelica protested, looking down at herself, drawing attention to her skimpy underwear.

"You don't need to worry about that," Masako said, grinning. "That's for Keahi to worry about, he's the wedding coordinator."

"And I want him to sing a wedding song for us," Carol said.

"He'll do it for our kids," Angelica added.

"Whose kids?" Masako asked, looking puzzled.

"Our kids," Angelica said. "The three of us—our kids."

Keahi could feel Masako staring at him in wonder. It took a lot of control for him to avoid her inquisitive eyes. Instead, he looked out the window and noted that it was going to be a bright, sunny day.

"So," Masako said to Keahi, "this means you are accepting my offer?"

"For one wedding, at least," he mumbled, turning his gaze to meet her eyes. "Then we'll see."

CHAPTER TWENTY-NINE

WALKING HOME FROM DUKE'S BAR, Keahi was composing a wedding song in his head for Angelica and Carol. He was unconsciously humming the melody, unaware of the curious looks from tourists.

He paused when he came to Gandhi's statue.

He reflected on Gandhi's marriage: Gandhi had married when he was thirteen years of age, still a child, yet eager to follow the guidance of his father, not knowing any better. Keahi tried to imagine the young Gandhi and his child bride sitting on a wedding *dias*, performing the *Saptapadi*, putting sweet *Kansar* into each other's mouths.

He looked up at Gandhi, scrutinized his bronze face.

"The sisters know what they are doing, *bhai*. They understand the significance of marriage."

Then he heard two gunshots; the second shot followed the first so closely it sounded like an echo.

His body flew off the ground and upwards onto the bronze legs of the statue. He held fast to a bronze sandal. He could not feel the ground beneath his feet.

"No," he mumbled, as he felt the strength in his hands bleed away.

His ears were ringing.

He felt a moment of confusion and fear and terror, followed by a moment of crystal clarity, then remorse.

I have wasted my life...

Clinging to the bronze foot of the Mahatma, he wanted to offer an apology. He wanted to say, "I'm so very sorry." But there was no one to hear.

A week after Keahi was murdered, Santos received an inter-office envelope containing a photo. It was addressed to "Williams" from the building manager, who included a short note: "Found by custodian in conference room 610." Not knowing where "Williams" worked, someone had attached a multi-branch route slip.

Santos laughed, then wept.

So Keahi never had the photo.

Santos placed it into a new envelope, which he addressed to the Captain and dropped in the mailbox at the side of the building.

That evening, while sitting in his recliner at home, he suffered a nervous breakdown. Employees who didn't know him started the rumor that he had suffered the breakdown because he'd had a close, personal relationship with Keahi. Nothing could have been further from the truth.

CHAPTER THIRTY

AT FIRST LIKO WAS RELUCTANT to accept Kwon's invitation to climb to the top of Diamond Head because he knew that Kwon had severe rheumatoid arthritis, and he didn't think Kwon understood how strenuous a climb it was to the top. But Kwon had insisted: "Tourists, kids, make the climb every day." So Liko accepted.

Liko had been right, though. Kwon was in no condition to climb. In addition to his arthritis, he was terribly out of shape. But Kwon persevered, and they climbed slowly up the trail, frequently resting on the switchbacks, until they reached the summit of the dead volcano, eventually.

At the top, sitting on a concrete observation platform, gazing out at Waikiki and the Pacific Ocean below them, Kwon produced two lukewarm bottles of water from his small backpack. He gave one to Liko and guzzled the other.

"Thanks," Liko said.

They took in the panoramic view of Kapiolani Park, the Waikiki Shell, the concrete hotels, and the Pacific Ocean.

The hotels looked like corncobs that had been broken into two or three pieces and then stuck upright into asphalt. The lanais covering the face of the buildings looked like recesses left by corn kernels that had been chewed off. The ocean was several shades of blue and green.

"Keahi said you used to be an astronomer."

"Yes. I was."

"So tell me," Liko waved his hand across the horizon, "where did all this come from?"

"From nothing. From pure, unadulterated, nothingness. Nothingness so pure that no human mind can fathom it."

"But *you* fathom it?" Liko asked, curious how Kwon would reply.

"I've studied theories. I've read cosmological papers."

"So how did it all get here?"

Kwon shrugged. "Before I left the university, I was interested in finding an answer. But now . . ."

Liko let him explain.

"Keahi and I used to argue about it. I can hear him now: 'Kwon, just because the universe began with a big, meaningless bang, doesn't mean that we are not special, both individually and as a species.' His argument had something to do with a theory of evolution that he believed in."

"Keahi and I never had a chance to talk about that," Liko said, his voice sad.

"He believed that evolution ties us all together, people and animals and plants. He believed there is a common bond between all living matter and all energy. He thought we are all part of some cosmic event that was being witnessed by our collective being, our minds, our imagination."

"You don't agree?"

Kwon shrugged his shoulders. "If it's an event, it is one without causal effect. That is what the mathematics of the big bang tells us."

"Don't you find that depressing?"

"Why?" Kwon asked.

"There must be something more," Liko said.

"Keahi thought that the first four billion years just laid the foundation for the next four billion. He told me once, 'Our species' best years are ahead of us.' He believed there was still a chance that we would evolve into something . . . something special." Kwon's voice broke. "He believed that our species' potential still lay ahead of us.'"

"What do you think?" Liko asked.

"It's possible."

"But it doesn't have to be?"

"That's correct."

They watched the bright orange glow of the setting sun flash green.

"So what do *you* believe?" Kwon asked.

"Life may be meaningless, but it still grabs you by the balls."

They watched the sunset fill the sky. They were both thinking of Keahi's memorial service, his ashes taken out on an outrigger canoe and scattered on the surface of the ocean he loved so much.

"It's time to hike down," Liko said. "They will close the park soon."

"I want to give you something first," Kwon said. He pulled an envelope out of his backpack and handed it to Liko.

"What is it?"

"The identity of the man who killed Keahi."

Liko snatched the envelope from Kwon and started to rip it open, but Kwon stopped him by placing his misshapen, arthritic hand on top of Liko's tanned hand.

"Please, don't open it now. Wait until you get back to your car."

"Who is it?"

"The man who lives next door to your great-aunt," Kwon said. "Isn't *that* ironic."

"The man she calls the Captain?"

"Yes, but his real name is Nobu Hashimoto."

Liko nodded.

"His name kept showing up on a list of landowners who had contaminated properties, and who had used Kalele's Lab. He belonged to several old land *huis*, too. I didn't make the connection at first because he changed his name. Of course he now has a new alias. Back then he was Nobu Hashimoto; today he is Shigaru Tagawa or the Captain."

"What do you know about him?"

"He owns a night club," Kwon added. "The Kesago Club."

Liko nodded again.

"And he has Ned."

Liko was stunned. His mouth dropped open.

"Yeah, he has little Ned," Kwon repeated. He paused long enough to control his emotions. His lower lip quivered, almost imperceptibly, but Liko saw it.

After a moment, Kwon cleared his throat, roughly. "Keahi had breakfast with this guy. He told me about it once. He asked Mr. Hashimoto about an underground storage tank in his club's parking lot, whether or not there had been a gasoline release into the soil. Mr. Hashimoto lied to him. I'm sure that it was gasoline from his property that caused the explosion at the child care center. His property is upgradient from the pet store, too." Kwon balled his arthritic hands into tight fists.

In a hushed tone Liko asked, "And Keahi never knew?" His body was tense.

Kwon opened his fists and laid his hands palm down on his thighs, steadying himself. "Keahi said that the Captain frequently went to the same restaurant. It's a lanai restaurant in a hotel in Waikiki."

Kwon paused, cleared his throat, and continued. "I wanted to see what this guy looked like. You understand? I wanted to know if I had ever seen him before." He lowered his voice and whispered, "I wanted to know who he was!"

He then resumed normal volume, although his hands were still trembling, "So, I went to the restaurant . . . last Friday . . . and waited for him to show up . . . for breakfast—"

"And?" Liko prompted.

"And I saw him. And that's when I saw Little Ned."

Liko lost color.

Kwon told Liko everything he knew about the Captain, including a feeling, no, more a prediction distilled from his research, that the Captain might hurt other members of the team at any moment, perhaps even Toi. Kwon concluded with, "It's all in that envelope."

Liko nodded, got to his feet, weakly, and slapped the brown envelope against his thigh.

Kwon remained seated.

"Aren't you coming down with me?"

"No. I'm going to stay here for a while."

Liko gave him a questioning look.

"I want to see the stars tonight."

CHAPTER
THIRTY-ONE

THE MOTION-SENSING LIGHTS in the Captain's back yard illuminated Liko. He braced himself for a perimeter alarm to sound, but it didn't and he allowed his nerves to relax a notch. He saw a video camera mounted under the eave, panning back and forth. Too late to hide. If it was recording then it already had his image.

But what an image!

He stood six feet five inches tall. He was wearing only a brown loincloth. His deeply tanned chest and his muscular shoulders shone in the moonlight. The Hawaiian war mask was a snug fit. And he carried a Hawaiian war club—a heavy koa club with large shark teeth set in a row on a massive ball of solid koa.

The ocean was in the background.

The police would look at the recording later and swear that the Hawaiian warrior arose from the ocean and then walked confidently—not crouching or sneaking about the grounds— but walked boldly to a window at the back of the main house.

Liko raised the club and tapped the windowpane. It exploded. Reaching in, he unlocked and opened the window, and then he climbed effortlessly into the mansion.

Still no alarm. Why isn't there an alarm?

He began to search the unfamiliar house, room by room, looking for little Ned.

He found Alegado watching a pornographic movie on a big screen high-definition television in the bar room, next to bottles of Chivas Regal and crosscut-patterned whiskey glasses and a bucket of ice, seated in a black leather chair, his hand on his privates.

Alegado saw the dark image of the war mask suddenly appear on the wall to the right of the television screen, silhouetted onto the wall by a light behind the warrior. Alegado jumped to his feet but was struck down with one smooth blow to the head, even before he had turned completely around. An almost fatal blow.

The warrior reached down and picked up a loose tooth that had flown out of Alegado's mouth. He placed it in a leather pouch on a cord around his neck.

Methodically, room by room, he searched the ground level. But he found no one else.

Taking the stairs, he climbed to the second floor.

In the first bedroom, he found Ned, asleep and alone. He quietly woke him, with his hand over his small mouth.

He was naked. Liko noticed that he had yellow and black bruises covering large areas of his small body—his neck, sides, and buttocks. His lower lip was puffy, too.

Liko fought back the tears that welled up in his eyes. He knew what had happened. Anger radiated from him like heat from a burning house.

He ripped off the top bed sheet, triple folded it, and wrapped it gently around Ned's petite body. He draped the remaining cloth onto Ned's narrow shoulders, toga-like.

Liko took him by the hand, led him out into the hall.

He systematically began to check each bedroom on both sides of the long hallway, opening each bedroom door, peering inside, crisscrossing his way down the long hallway. The first three rooms were empty.

He found himself standing in front of a bedroom door that had a clown's face on the door, hanging at waist level. He ran his hand across the face: the hair was orange yarn, the eyes dull-white macaroni, the smile textured sand. It was a large, frightening, smiling face of a clown.

He turned the doorknob. As he started to push open the door, Ned grabbed his hand. Ned's wide eyes revealed his fear and pleaded with Liko to stop.

With the large palm of his free hand he pushed Ned gently, yet firmly against the opposite wall of the narrow hallway. Then he stepped back to the clown-faced door. He turned the doorknob, looked back at Ned, saw the fear in his eyes, raised the war club overhead, and cracked open the door. He peered inside.

It was dark. Darker than the other rooms in the house. There were no window in this room. Or perhaps the window had been sealed shut. No light except the dim light that now entered from the hallway through the cracked door.

Liko's eyes adjusted and then he saw the figure of a small boy asleep in a small bed. He looked peaceful. Liko started to enter, intending to help this boy escape, too, but then a small hand gripped his loincloth and tugged. He looked down and saw terror flashing across Ned's face.

Ned's small head shook side-to-side, pleading with Liko not to enter.

Liko paused and looked across the room at the sleeping boy. The boy appeared okay—for the present moment anyway. Why was Ned so excited? Liko had no idea. But then he reasoned that he didn't need to be encumbered by a second boy if he stumbled into a body guard or even the Captain, so he made a quick decision to leave the sleeping boy behind for now. So he quietly closed the door.

The door clicked closed.

He took Ned's small hand in his left hand. He let the war club hang by his right side: twenty pounds of heavy koa wood and shark's teeth. Together they checked the remaining rooms along the hallway, one by one, finding nothing.

After that, Liko decided that they should leave. He retraced his steps down the hallway, and then, together, they descended the stairs to the first level and returned to the back of the mansion. He was still leading Ned by the hand.

Instead of exiting through the window, he thought that it would be easier for Ned to leave through the back door, which they did. And that took them past the pool area. And that's where they discovered the Captain. In fact, Liko walked right up to the Captain, was right on top of him, before he saw him in the shadows, asleep in a lounge chair beside his large quiet pool.

So that's why the alarm didn't sound: the master of the house is outside by his pool, and he turned off the alarm. A stupid mistake.

Liko quietly walked Ned around a large chair, then leaned over and whispered, firmly: "Stay behind this chair. Don't move. You understand?"

Ned looked up at him with frightened eyes and nodded.

"Turn around. Close your eyes."

Ned obeyed. He turned around, squatted, and hunched his little body into a ball.

"Cover your ears."

Ned obeyed, cupped his hands over his ears.

"Now don't move," Liko whispered.

He looked down at Ned. He was just a boy, a little boy.

Then Liko turned his attention back to the Captain; he walked over and kicked him in the leg.

The Captain stirred, woke up, tried to sit up. His elbow slipped on the narrow lounge armrest and he fell back into his cushy chair.

He was drunk.

That angered Liko. He wanted the Captain to see the club as he swung it down on his head. But he was too drunk. Damn him!

Fuming with anger, Liko swung the club across the Captain's knees, the shark's teeth slicing through his flesh. A spray of red blood whipped across the pool deck, painting a red trail.

The Captain's eyes opened in terror! He yelled.

Yes, Liko thought. *That is the reaction I want.*

He swung again, striking the Captain across his stomach.

Then he felt a tug at his shirt. He glanced downward and saw Ned at his side.

Ned reached for the club.

Liko was stunned. His eyes narrowed as he looked from Ned to the Captain, then back to Ned. Ned's swollen lower lip trembled. And Liko recognized not fear, but anger.

Liko understood, clearly, and he gave Ned the club.

It was almost too heavy for the boy, but he was determined.

He drug it—white shark teeth scraping black slate. He raised it with both hands but it fell back on his small shoulder. The sharp teeth dug into the toga bed sheet. He struggled to get the weight under control, wrapping both of his small hands around the wooden handle.

He swung it over his head and brought it down on the Captain, striking his right elbow. Liko heard the bone crack and the Captain yelled. He yelled again and again as Ned swung down on him, fierce and brutal: again and again, breaking his other arm and then breaking both his legs.

Ned took the full measure of his revenge. He exhausted his rage. And then he stopped.

The Captain was still breathing.

Liko reached down and collected several of the Captain's teeth and put them in the small leather pouch with Alegado's molar. Then he grabbed the Captain by a foot.

The video cameras recorded the events that followed. A Hawaiian warrior dragged the Captain's body by his heel around the perimeter of the pool to the barbecue pit. The silhouette of a small boy dressed in a toga followed close behind him, black against the ocean and the moon, which was low on the horizon.

The Hawaiian warrior picked up the unconscious Captain, raised his broken body high overhead, and turned slowly in the moonlight, one hundred and eighty degrees. He dropped the Captain onto his genuflected knee, breaking his back. Now bundled, he lowered the body onto the rock grill.

The Captain moved. He was still alive, though there was a huge wound in his shoulder, bleeding profusely—his shoulder and body almost severed.

The warrior searched the grill until he found a box of long stick matches in a *puka* built into the rock.

He turned the gas on. He took a match slowly out of the box and—

There was a tug at his loincloth.

Liko looked down and saw Ned shake his head side-to-side.

"Ah, little Wiglaf!" he said. "You want to light the gas?"

But instead, with a twist of a knob, Ned turned it off.

Astonished, Liko reached down and took Ned's small hand. It would be as the boy wished.

Liko decided not to go back into the house for the child asleep in the bedroom. It was unnecessary. The child was safe now, no longer in danger.

The next day, when the police looked at the video footage, they swore that the Hawaiian warrior and the boy had walked into the ocean, hand-in-hand. But it was only an optical effect caused by the slope of the yard down to the ocean.

Instead, Liko and the old fisherman's great-grandson had climbed over the wall and down through the bougainvillea to the great-aunt's backyard.

After changing into his own clothes, Liko wiped the war club clean and returned it to the glass display case. He carefully set the war mask on the top glass shelf and closed the glass door.

Next he opened another display case and removed a koa bowl. He ran his hand over its smooth, shiny surface and the rough, inlaid teeth. Then he took a small knife out of his trousers and sat down. Ned sat at his feet, resting his head on Liko's leg, as Liko slowly carved the hard koa wood. After fifteen minutes, he had made two small holes.

He took two teeth out of the pouch hung around his neck and inserted them into the *pukas*, working them into the wood. The molar still had blood on it. He spat and wiped it clean with his fingers, rubbing the tooth and the surrounding wood with his shirt tail until the wood looked shined. Then he gently moved Ned's head off his leg—Ned had fallen asleep—and returned the bowl to the display case.

After Liko and Ned left the next day, the great-aunt stood in front of the display case, staring at the bowl and the two new, shiny teeth set into its base among the other molars and premolars. She took the war club out of the case and sprayed it with lemon-scented Pledge and cleaned off all bloody traces of the horrific events of the night. She also cleaned the red splatter off the war mask. After she was satisfied all was clean, she firmly closed the display and locked it.

She held the key tightly in her hand as she walked up the staircase, past the landing and the display of Keahi's antique musical instruments, which had been returned to her after his murder. She stopped her ascent long enough to look out the window. The moon had set into the ocean.

ABOUT THE AUTHOR

Greg Olmsted is an environmental health specialist. He served thirty-three years in environmental health programs. Olmsted hopes to use the arts to increase public awareness of environmental and public health issues. He resides with his wife in Washington, DC.